A stint in highway design is what gave author William Hallstead the idea for THE MAN DOWNSTAIRS, the story of a young draftsman in a city highway department. "A lot of today's young people are going to be faced with the very same pressures that confront Don," he predicts.

Mr. Hallstead's first love was aviation. He has been a civil flight instructor, glider pilot, crop duster, and author of several books (including ghosting some Hardy Boys titles) and articles on the subject of flying. In addition, he has been a publisher, public-relations director, director of development for a Maryland TV network, and a dealer in miniatures. He and his wife live in Clarks Summit, Pennsylvania, and have two grown children.

THE MAN DOWNSTAIRS

Also by William F. Hallstead
Ghost Plane of Backwater

THE MAN DOWNSTAIRS

by

William F. Hallstead

Elsevier/Nelson Books
New York

PZ4
H 193
Man
1979

No character in this book is intended to represent any actual person; all the incidents of the story are entirely fictional in nature.

Library of Congress Cataloging in Publication Data

Hallstead, William F
    The man downstairs.

    SUMMARY: In the midst of corrupt city politics, a young civil servant refuses to go along with "the way it's always been."
    I. Title.
PZ4.H193Man   [PS3558.A395]   813'.5'4   79–4061
ISBN 0–525–66628–1

Published in the United States by Elsevier/Nelson Books, a division of Elsevier-Dutton Publishing Company, Inc., New York. Published simultaneously in Don Mills, Ontario, by Thomas Nelson and Sons (Canada) Limited.

Printed in the U.S.A.   First Edition
10 9 8 7 6 5 4 3 2 1

THE MAN
DOWNSTAIRS

CHAPTER 1

THE MEMO gave Don Ellison a sick twist in the middle of his chest. I'm being stupid, he told himself. It's only another memo from downstairs. But he was good at spotting trouble, and somehow he knew that this innocent-looking mimeographed message meant just that. Yet if anyone in the drafting room had told Don at that moment that he was about to get into the worst mess in his twenty years of life, he would have laughed out loud.

On this early-summer afternoon, the loftlike drafting room seemed more of a refuge than a potential storm center. Once you nailed down a job here, you could quietly design streets and avenues for the city of Millbury until you were as old as white-haired Al Hill over there.

"Voluntary contribution" were the key words in the memo. Voluntary? The old hands here in the second-floor drafting room of the Department of Streets knew how voluntary the contribution was going to be. So did the administrative people downstairs. So did the head of the department, Carleton J. Munroe, "The Man Downstairs." He knew best of all, because he had written the thing.

On the drafting stool beside Don, Gil Barber grunted. "See? Just like I told you. You didn't believe me when I said this was coming, Don buddy. We're going to be hit. You still think you and Sue are going to get out of Millbury next year like you planned?"

"We'll get out. Just as soon as I've got two years of street design under my belt here. I told you, Consolidated Engineering promised me a job just as soon as I'm qualified."

"From beginning draftsman to street designer in two short years? That'll be the day!"

"I can make it."

"Can you eat dirt here for eighteen months more? That's what's going to do you in, buddy."

"I've lasted six so far."

"Yeah, but the political season has just opened." Gil flicked his copy of the memo with his forefinger. "The money gunners are loose. Even if you last another year and a half, you won't have enough dough saved up to move across the street, let alone move out of state to Consolidated."

Gil had a point there, Don conceded silently. He and Sue had just begun to learn that being married costs money. They always needed something. No matter how hard both of them tried to sock away a few dollars, the money just seemed to melt through their fingers. They were pinching pennies so hard that Lincoln had a concussion. Even when Don's draftsman's pay was supplemented by income from Sue's receptionist job, it was almost impossible to save much.

Now, though, things had begun to look just a shade better. No matter what Sue's mother and father had thought about their ability to survive, so far they had made it okay. And they had made it on their own. Sue had answered a classified ad in the *Millbury Chronicle* and now had a job with Castleton Printing. Don had found his job through the classified columns of the same paper, too, and he'd landed it without any help from anybody. Well, almost. No matter what your ability and experience, to get a city job you had to have a "sponsor"—someone fairly prominent in the political party in power.

Don's parents lived on a farm ten miles out of Millbury, and his dad had made it a point to steer clear of politics. He wanted no part of "big-city crookedness," as he called it, and Don had left home under a cloud. So Sue's father had gotten a friend of his—some city councilman—to sign Don's application for the city job. No problem.

"Oh, well," Gil Barber said abruptly, "scratch up the money, pay off, and you're home safe." His blocky face wore a wry little smile.

"It says 'voluntary,' " Don pointed out. "What if I don't pay it?"

"Hold back on a handout for the politicians' campaign kitty in an election year? You've got to be kidding!"

Don pushed back his forelock of dark hair, and his face twisted into a scowl. "But it says 'voluntary,' " he insisted.

"Come on. I told you that's a code word. There isn't anything voluntary about this. You either give, or The Man Downstairs will send up your walking papers."

"I doubt it."

"Don't doubt it a quarter of an inch worth, Donny boy. What this little memo message really says is, 'You will kick back a piece of your salary to the party.' Period."

"That's illegal."

"Not if it's called a voluntary contribution. You get the picture?"

Don picked up his pencil and tapped its blunt end against his teeth. "How long has this little custom been going on?"

"Who knows? I've paid it every time there's been an election for the past four years. It's part of life if you want to work for this city."

"But nobody can force anyone to pay to keep his job, Gil."

"Brother, are you a lamb in a wolf's den! Just keep quiet and pay up when the time comes. That's my advice, and if you're only half smart, you'll take it."

"I can't believe they get away with—"

"Cool it. Here comes Corrigan."

Marty Corrigan cruised between the rows of drafting tables like a battleship maneuvering through a narrow channel. His belly strained for freedom against his blue shirt. The drafting supervisor was a huge man, a straight line from his heels to the back of his close-cropped head, but his stomach stuck out like a sagging sack of dough.

"You two got a problem?" he rumbled.

"Everything's under control, Marty," Gil said with a quick grin.

"See it stays that way, me boys. The Conklin Street redesign's got to be out of here in no more'n a month. Bear down on them cross-section sheets."

"Call them out," Gil muttered.

4

Don picked up the hardbound field-survey book. "Station sixty. Center-line elevation is three-four-seven-four-one . . ."

Gil began to plot the survey data on the green-lined cross-section sheet from which they would later compute cut-and-fill yardage.

Don called the numbers mechanically, his mind going back to their pre-Corrigan conversation. Salary kickback—and Gil accepted it!

". . . Ten feet left, elevation three-four-five-point-five-six. . . ."

He watched the stocky red-haired draftsman mark the elevation points with neat pencil dots. Gil's green eyes were intent on the cross-section sheet, but when Corrigan had ambled to the far side of the drafting room, those eyes would dart mischievously toward Don with a new joke or a wisecrack that would come close to breaking up both of them. Gil was a free-thinking jokester, surely not a willing payer of kickback money.

Don remembered his first day on the job last December, when he began to learn the work he was doing now. After three hours of reading the monotonous stadia shots, he had looked up in exasperation. "You want to know something? For this kind of work, they could have gone out in the street and grabbed the first guy who came along."

Gil had stared at him solemnly and said, "You want to know something? They did."

That had melted the ice, and they had become close friends, though they weren't really close in age. Gil at twenty-six had served two years in the Navy and seemed to be a pretty sharp character. Don had gone out of high school into two years of knocking around in a variety of low-caliber jobs: gas-station attendant, lifeguard at the city-park pool, then a back-busting eight months with a highway-construction company up on Bald Mountain.

That had really been a rough one. In the middle of it, he had met Sue Wallace. After a few months, he knew he wanted to marry her. Her folks thought they were crazy to marry so young. So did his, but they weren't so noisy about it.

Even Gil still chipped away at him occasionally. "You didn't have to marry her to get what you wanted. Haven't you heard of women's lib? Don't you know it's the single man's answer to wedding bells? Ask Lila. She feels the same way." Lila Greenwood more or less lived with Gil. At least it looked that way to Don, although tall, cool Lila never matched Gil's big talk about it. She never said much of anything at all.

"Sue stands up for what she thinks is right," Don had countered. "We both think that if we love each other, we ought to have the guts to make a legal commitment."

"Yeah, sure. You get around like I have, see a few things, get your eyes opened, you'll learn to take what you can get without tying yourself down."

No matter what Gil thought, Don had found marriage a good thing so far. No more loneliness. Lots of loving.

"Call those stadia shots," Gil rasped in his ear. "Old Corrigan's giving us the fish eye again."

"Station sixty-three plus fifty. Centerline three-four-nine-point-one-six. . . ." Don looked at his watch. "Hey, it's nearly four thirty. Let's get out of here."

They spread the black cloth covers over their tables and became part of the crowd of engineers and draftsmen who shuffled down the wide steps to the double-doored entrance of the old converted school building. The outside heat hit them like a soft wall.

"You're sure quiet for a guy who just got off work on a Friday," Gil said as they reached the parking lot. "What's eating you?"

Don slipped the key into the door of his five-year-old Ford. "You were kidding, weren't you?"

"About what?"

"About the kickback."

"You'll find out how much I was kidding. I told you, it's part of working here. Consider it club dues."

"No, it's not like dues, Gil. It's crooked."

"Life is crooked."

Don looked at him squarely. "Not everyone's."

"Listen to the saint! Don boy, don't fight it. You'll pay up just like we all do."

CHAPTER 2

DON LOVED Sue's jumpy walk. The blond bouncer, he called her. Nothing bothered his girl. She cared about people and could always see something good in everyone. She had hair the color of sunflower petals, soft brown eyes, a sunny smile. The top of her head barely reached his shoulder. He was proud of his wife.

The words sent a warm rush through him. He was lean and plain. She was lively and could be friendly with anyone. He was quiet, and maybe—he could admit it to himself—maybe he was even a little hard to know.

"How did a sad-eyed hungry hound dog like you ever latch on to a honey like her?" Gil had burst out when Don had first introduced him to Sue. Don couldn't have given him the answer. He didn't know what Sue saw in him. He just considered himself the luckiest guy in Millbury, and he knocked himself out to keep a good thing going. Another year and a half with the Department of Streets, then there'd be no holding back the two of them.

He pulled the Ford off Mill Street into the parking area in front of the white-painted cinderblock Castleton Printing Company Building. On the dot of five, Castleton employees began to come out. Some pressmen still wore their handmade square paper hats that kept printing ink out of their hair. Offset cameramen, who worked in darkrooms most of the day, squinted into the sun. Office girls chatted about their dates. Then came Sue, in a pale-blue pantsuit that set off the gold of her close-cut hair.

"Hi! " She leaned through the open window and kissed him, her lips warm and soft, then trotted around to the passenger's side. "Have a good day?"

"So-so. How about you?"

"Not exciting, but every dollar counts. Why 'so-so'? I thought you learned something new every day. That's the idea, isn't it?"

"I sure learned something new today." He eased the old two-door back into traffic. Why had he said a dumb thing like that? She'd never let it pass, and he hadn't wanted to worry her.

"Don?"

He glanced sideways at her. "What?"

"I asked you what was upsetting you, and you didn't answer, hon."

He hadn't even heard her. "It's okay. It's nothing."

"It can't be nothing. Come on, honey."

He'd let the polecat stick its nose out of the bag, and there was no way to push it back in. "They sent a notice around asking for a voluntary contribution to the party."

"What party?"

"Democrat, Republican, whichever one is in power at the moment. They both do it."

She frowned. "But if it's voluntary, what's so awful?"

"Gil says it really isn't voluntary. You give, or you're out."

"Oh, come on. Gil always has some wild story to tell." She pointed. "There's that Chinese place. Let's take home some egg rolls, and I'll make some spaghetti—"

"Egg rolls and spaghetti?" She could come up with some of the wildest menus.

"Sure. *Ciao mein!*" She wrote the two words on a piece of paper and held it in front of him. He laughed. Then her face clouded. "Oh, heck. I just remembered. Hobie Hasfeld is coming over for supper tonight."

"Well, he doesn't stay around long. And he eats whatever we offer him. Newspapermen aren't particular, I guess. Must be their weird hours."

"I'll buy," Sue offered. "I got paid today." She reached for her handbag.

"Keep your money, woman. Besides, we'll need it Monday for the apartment rent." He swung into the parking area of the Ho-Ho Chinese Take-Out and came out five minutes later with a white bag. They were on their way again.

She snuggled against him. "Did you know that the smell of fried food drives me absolutely wild?"

"Later, Sue, later." He wished he could share her lightheartedness, but an uncomfortable lump was building inside him—the cold nervousness he got when he didn't know exactly what was going to go wrong, although he couldn't shake the feeling that something would.

"Stupid." It was stupid.

Sue's head came up sharply. "What's stupid?"

Had he actually said it out loud?

She moved away and looked at him. "Don, honey, what's really wrong?"

"It's that contribution thing. I can't get it out of my mind."

She slid back to him and deepened her voice. "So my man can't get a big worry out of his mind, huh? If Hobie leaves as soon as he usually does, it's early to bed, Worry Wart."

Hobie Hasfeld waited on the front steps of their Timberlane apartment unit, leaning against the bricks beside the doorway. "You know this place needs paint?"

"This place needs a lot of things," Don said as they shook hands, "but we are trying to save for a place of our own."

"I know what you mean. I'm having my own problems with personal economics. Sometimes I wish I had a working partner like this girl of yours, Don. Hi, Sue. What're we eating?"

"Surprise. Come on, help me get the spaghetti sauce underway."

"I thought it was a surprise."

"That's in the bag."

After they had eaten, Don watched Hobie help Sue with the dishes. He was a big guy. He'd been big as long as Don remembered him, which went way back to the fifth or sixth grade at Millbury Elementary. That was when they'd first become friends. Hobie was like a clumsy bear: hair down to his collar, which was never combed more than a couple of licks, bushy black mustache hanging past the corners of his wide mouth,

11

little laughing eyes deep under caterpillar eyebrows. He stood, sat, and walked with his shoulders hunched as if he were still part of the Millbury High football team offensive line.

"Will you look at the lord of the manor lounging there slurping coffee!" Hobie boomed. "Pouring it down, while we two do all the work."

"You volunteered," Don pointed out. His voice held an unintended edge.

"Hey, what's eating you? I'm just funning, old buddy. You weren't exactly sparkling through dinner, either, come to think of it. What's the word?"

Should he tell Hobie? The guy was a friend, but he was a newspaperman, too, even though he'd been at it only a few months.

Sue in her naiveté took the decision away from Don. "It's some silly thing at the office. They've asked everybody for some kind of contribution."

Hobie dried his hands on the dish towel. "What kind of contribution?"

"Forget it, Hobie. It's nothing."

"Oh, nothing!" Sue put in. "He's been moping about it since he heard."

Hobie draped the towel over the rack beneath the sink and straddled a chair. "Come on, buddy, tell old Hobie your problem."

What did Don see in those close-set little eyes? Interest, sure. But was it interest in a friend's problem or interest in a possible story? Had three months with the *Chronicle* been enough to make Hobie a reporter first and a friend second?

Don took a long breath. "Maybe I'm making too much out of it."

"Let me decide that."

"Well . . . they sent us a memo today."

"And?"

"And it said that we are expected to make a voluntary contribution to the party."

"You got this memo somewhere?"

"As a matter of fact, I have." Don reached into his shirt pocket.

Hobie smoothed the sheet on the kitchen table, studied it, and his eyebrows hiked up. "Could be nothing. Could be something."

"Depending on what?"

"On what happens to you if you don't kick in like they ask." He looked down at the memo again. "Can I keep this?"

"Why?"

"I've heard about this sort of thing going on in city departments, but I've never seen it on paper before."

"But you just said it could be nothing," Sue put in, turning from the sink with a sponge in her hand. "Now you sound like maybe it really is something to worry about."

"If Don refuses to contribute and that refusal results in any prejudice toward him on the part of the Department of Streets, then I think that might be a violation of a state version of the Hatch Act."

"You're talking like a lawyer," Sue said.

"I'm thinking like a newspaperman. For a change, I'd have a big story."

"Wait a minute, wait a minute," Don broke in. "That sounds like you want me to make some sort of test case out of this thing."

"Look, you don't sound to me like you're exactly pleased with this 'innocent' little memo. And it actually is innocent, you know. It's worded very carefully."

"Gil Barber doesn't think it's so harmless."

"He ought to know. He's been working for the city for a while." Hobie caught Don's glance and held it. "Just what did Gil say?"

"That there's a kickback system, all right. This memo's just the opening shot."

Hobie leaned back, and a grin spread across his face. "Old buddy, you and I could have a real time with this one!"

"Now hold on. Don't go making a test case out of me! You know I'm no more of a crusader than the next guy."

"I know you're a little more conscientious than the next guy, though. Remember that little Halloween deal five or six years ago, when the rest of us figured out how to put old man Hacker's tire display over the school flagpole like donuts on a spike? You wouldn't have any part of that because his wife was sick."

"But I didn't turn any of you in, did I? He had to cut those tires off, and he never knew who was responsible for the prank. I didn't hurt him, but I didn't help him, either. How moral was I, Hobie?"

"We were kids then."

"Does a couple of years make us that much smarter?"

"Oh, stop it!" Sue said. "Hobie, leave him alone. He's not going to get into trouble just so you can write a story."

Hobie stood up and shoved his hands into his pockets. "Terrific, Sue. Aren't we the same people who spent so much time knocking the older generation because they wouldn't get involved? What about all our lip service about caring for people?"

14

"We were kids," Sue said, unintentionally echoing Hobie. "It was easier then."

"Sure it was easier," he shot back. "That's the whole point. It's simple enough to solve problems that you don't have yourself. Now Don's got one, and it's not easy at all."

"Come on," Don said. "What do you expect me to do?"

"What do *I* expect you to do? What kind of question is that? It's not my problem. It's yours."

"Oh, that's a great stand to take," Sue cut in. "First you lecture Don on his lack of concern for people, then you back out of it yourself. What kind of friend are you? And why is it so terrible anyway if Don is asked for a contribution?"

Hobie held up a beefy left hand and ticked off points with the forefinger of his right. "One, the city might be violating a law. Two, Don's going along with it would help that violation to go on and on. Three, if he does go along with it, he'll be just another schlunk in a crooked system. That's what's so terrible, Sue."

She stared at him, then lowered her eyes. "Somehow it doesn't seem worth all this argument."

"I'm sure it doesn't seem worth it to other city employees. That's why they just shut up and put up."

"Maybe that's what I should do, too, Hobie."

"Damn it, Don! That's exactly what you shouldn't do. I'll tell you this: if you give in, you're a part of it."

"And you'd have no story."

"Maybe not. But you'd have lost more than I'd lose."

Sue bristled. "That's not fair! Not fair at all."

"Maybe it isn't. Maybe I'm trying too hard for headlines." He glanced up at the kitchen clock. "Look,

15

I've got to go to work. Promise me one thing, will you, ol' buddy? Keep me up on what's happening. Okay?"

"So you can keep the paper up on it?"

"I swear I won't print a line without your go-ahead. Fair enough?" He thrust out his huge paw.

Don nodded, and they shook hands hard. "Fair enough, Hobie."

Later, as he and Sue lay side by side, her voice came out of the darkness. "Don, before you do anything about that thing at work—"

"What do you mean, do anything?"

"Well, you either have to pay or not pay, don't you?"

She was right. There was no getting around it.

"Before you do, please let me talk to Daddy."

He fought back sudden anger. "Honey, I'm old enough to make decisions on my own."

She propped her head on an elbow and trailed her fingers across his chest. "But you're not a lawyer."

He was silent.

"Don, please. For me."

He let out a long sigh. "Ah-h, all right." Then he reached for her and pulled her toward him. "Come here, Sue!" He buried his face in the clean soap smell of her hair, but he couldn't shake that nagging cold lump that had come home with him. Hobie had been no help at all. The big clown had only convinced Don that things weren't going to add up to a picnic.

16

CHAPTER 3

CHIEF ENGINEER Charlie Pegler looked like a boy of the1940's grown old. He probably hadn't put on a pound since his days at State University School of Engineering. He still wore World War II haircuts, with the back of his neck and the sides almost shaved, and a gray lock tumbling over his forehead.

He leaned across Don's drafting table. "I'd like to talk with you in my office."

His voice was conversational. That was the way Pegler was: friendly and informal, like a small-town store owner. But something about him this morning sent a little chill through Don. He shrugged at Gil behind Pegler's back, put down his drawing pencil and followed the chief engineer to his little glass-enclosed office at the far end of the drafting room. They passed Billy Crimm on the way in, the big guy at the little desk just outside Pegler's office. Don often wondered exactly what Crimm did.

"Have a chair, Don." Pegler lifted a skinny hip up on his office table stacked with reference books and sat sidesaddle, one leg dangling. He pulled a pipe out of his shirt pocket and began to load it from a yellowing plastic pouch on the table.

"You're pretty new around here, so I think I owe you a few pointers." He put down the pouch, fished a lighter out of a shirt pocket, and flicked it until he had coaxed up a flame. Suck . . . puff. Suck . . . puff. The pipe finally took hold and the office was layered with smoke.

"A few pointers," he repeated. "You know that memo we all got Friday?"

"About a contribution." Pegler might act casual, Don thought, but he sure had a way of getting right to the point.

"A voluntary contribution, yes. Strictly routine, Don. Nothing to worry about. Only happens in election years." He gave Don a thin smile. "Sort of dues, you might call it."

"That's what Gil called it."

Pegler chuckled. "Gil Barber is a fella with the right idea."

"How much?" Don said. He wasn't smiling, and the chief engineer's little laugh died.

"Only a nominal amount."

Something about this fatherly approach was irritating. "What's a nominal amount?" Don's voice had taken on more hardness than he'd intended.

"Look, Don, I don't enjoy doing this. It's just that I'm the supervising engineer for the drafting room. The Man Downstairs sends up word through me. I feel like hell laying it on you fellows, but it's just something we all have to put up with."

"I make a hundred and twenty-five a week," Don said, "and I think I earn every penny of it."

"I know you do. You've got a lot on the ball."

"How much are you asking me to give back?"

In the silence, Pegler frowned. "Look, please understand something here. It's not me that's asking. I have to give, too. More than you."

Don's fingers tightened on the chair arms. "How much do I have to kick in, Mr. Pegler?"

The chief engineer's mouth was a grim line. He swung his head slowly from side to side. "You've got to understand the system. I told you, it's not me that's—"

"How much?"

"Four percent. At your pay level, that's only five dollars a week."

"But it's based on a whole year, isn't it? That's two hundred and sixty dollars!"

Pegler puffed his pipe, squinting at the brown linoleum floor. "Don, I wish I only had to give that much." He slumped forward, chewing on the pipestem. Then he suddenly straightened. "Now listen to me. The Man Downstairs wants one hundred percent cooperation. Take my advice. Pay your share, then forget it. It won't kill you."

Two hundred and sixty dollars. He supposed he and Sue could scrape it together somehow. Their pitiful little savings account would be wiped out, and they'd still have to find a hundred from somewhere else.

Yet the money wasn't the whole problem. Nobody seemed to understand that but Hobie. This was wrong! Why should he be forced to pay out money to keep his job?

"Mr. Pegler—"

The chief engineer looked up with something close to

distress across his thin face. "Don, hold it a minute." He stood and shut the office door. "I know how you feel. I know exactly how you feel. I was about your age when I started here. Long time ago. More years than I care to count. I came in with all the great ideas I think you have boiling inside you right now. Going to devote your life to public service, right?"

Not quite right, but they understood each other.

"Then I found out what it actually was going to cost me—not really a whole lot of money, when you get down to it. Oh, it hurt a little. It still pinches the old wallet sometimes. But now I plan for it. Used to be political bull roasts or clambakes. At first they cost only twenty-five bucks a ticket. Then they went to fifty, then a hundred.

"That's still less than—"

"Not for a table of six. But I just figured it as a cost of getting ahead. Every job has its price. In a private company, you might have to drive the boss's wife to the company picnic or buy your department supervisor a big Christmas present. It's just the cost of keeping the job you want."

Pegler leaned against the doorjamb, puffed his pipe, and gazed at the floor. He cleared his throat. "You follow me?"

"I understand you, Mr. Pegler."

"Then it's all straightened out."

"I understand *you*. I'm not sure I understand myself yet. What we're talking about is wrong, isn't it?"

"Wrong?"

"Against the law. Isn't taking money from government employees illegal?"

"It isn't illegal for employees to contribute money to political parties of their choice, Don. That's the point."

"Suppose my choice happens to be the other party?"

Pegler raised an eyebrow at him. "Don't kid me. I saw who sponsored your job application. A city councilman and a good party man. Look, you don't have to pay right away. The Man Downstairs doesn't turn in the department's contribution until August. If you're pushed for cash, you've got time to put it together."

"From where, Mr. Pegler?"

"Well, that's a problem a lot of us have. Nothing new about needing money, is there? You'll find a way, like the rest of us do. Now go on back to your work. We've held up that Conklin Street job long enough."

Don put his hand on the doorknob.

"Just a minute. Like you to do a little something for me." Pegler pulled a flat package out from under the reference table. "Tack these up around the area you live in, will you?"

There were a dozen more such parcels under the table, wrapped in brown paper.

"Just some posters for Sid Harte," Pegler explained. "He's running to keep his seat as city councilman. The Man Downstairs is a particular friend of his."

"But I'm not."

"Now look, Don. I thought we understood each other. You help the department, the department helps you."

This was wrong, too, Don thought. Why should I tack up Harte's posters just because I work for the city? But Pegler's tone had an edge that warned Don not to push further. Besides, putting up a few posters wasn't much of a commitment.

"Okay, I'll take the posters."

He felt the eyes of half the department on him as he

walked back to the drafting table with the package under his arm. The brown paper didn't fool anybody. Everyone knew what he had. Probably most of them had already been asked to tack up their own twenty-five or so, and those who hadn't been asked soon would be.

Gil Barber greeted him with a tight grin, nodding as if he'd known all along what was going to happen in Pegler's office.

"Got to you, didn't he? The old put-up-a-couple-of-posters game. I thought you were going to be the one guy who held out."

"Sticking up a handful of posters isn't the same as kicking in money."

"But it's giving in to the system, smart guy. You've just sold a little piece of yourself, and you're not even smart enough to bleed."

Don swung onto his drafting stool. "I didn't give away anything. Not like you. They say 'Jump,' and all you say is, 'How high?' "

"Listen to the chief of the resistance movement sitting there with the enemy's posters in his lap. What do you suppose the rest of the guys think now?"

"The rest of what guys?"

"The ones who'd like to break the back of this crooked system."

Don propped the package of posters against the table leg. "I didn't know there really were any others."

"Of course there are. There always are. They just don't speak up about it like you because they're smarter than you are."

"Or more scared."

"If you aren't scared, it's because you're too dumb to be scared. It's not just your couple of hundred bucks at

22

stake here. If you were somehow to manage to get all this dirty underwear out on a public washline, you'd lose your job, sure. But there'd be a chain reaction. I figure The Man Downstairs would get it right along with Pegler and everybody in between." Gil picked up a triangle and drew a line on his cross-section sheet. "Now does it finally begin to penetrate your thick skull why there can be a huge hassle over this little balk of yours?"

"Maybe it's time for a housecleaning," Don said, but to his surprise his voice had lost its punch.

Gil nodded. "Uh-uh. The old nerve is finally wavering, isn't it? Good thing, too. There's too much at stake in all this to make your kind of move healthy. It's just not worth it, buddy. Shut up and pay, or start checking shadows when you're walking alone."

Don forced a laugh. "Come on, Gil. You're talking like the TV Late Show. That kind of stuff doesn't happen today."

"And politicians don't break into the other party's offices, and no President tried to cover up corruption, right?"

Don tapped his drafting pencil on the table. This was Millbury, quiet old Millbury. Things like that couldn't happen here. Could they?

CHAPTER 4

WALTER WALLACE, Sue's father, bent over his patio barbeque grill. He was a nervous chef, who poked and flipped the hamburgers as if close attention would make them cook faster.

"Sorry I was late getting home," he apologized to Sue, Don, and his wife. He was an unsmiling man, not quite so tall as Don and a few pounds lighter; he was thin and graying, and seemed held together by nervous energy.

Don felt neutral toward his father-in-law. Except for Sue, they'd never found enough in common to get friendly about. Don was sure that Walter Wallace secretly felt his daughter could have done better and maybe worse. At any rate Walter Wallace seemed neutral toward Don, as well.

"I thought the jury was expected to reach a verdict early today, Walter." Elizabeth Wallace watched her husband as if she were afraid he would embarrass her by not answering. She was a heavy woman in her late forties but still pretty in a well-fed way. Her bouffant hair was always hairdresser perfect, an ash-gray bubble, spray set until it was windproof.

"Walter?" she prompted.

"Uh? Oh, they disagreed over some technical thing. Verdict didn't come in until late this afternoon. I nearly missed getting here altogether." He flipped over the hanburgers one last time, then leaned down to squint at them. "There, that does it. Everybody get a plate. Let's dig in."

Don was halfway through his second helping of potato salad when he realized Sue was trying to catch his eye across the patio. Her mouth formed the words, *Ask him.* She and Don had made a bet on what Sue's father would say.

"Mr. Wallace," Don began.

"It's Walter, Don."

But Sue's father wasn't really a first-name type.

'I want to ask you about something that came up at work."

"Ask away."

Don glanced at Sue. "Well, I'd like your opinion on something."

"That's what lawyers do best. Go ahead and state your case."

"It's not a case," Don said clumsily. "At least, not yet. What it is, well—"

"Oh, for heaven's sake!" Sue burst out. "They want him to make a contribution to the party, and he thinks it's wrong. Is it wrong, Daddy?"

She shot a glance at Don. Sometimes her readiness to speak out irritated him. This was one of the times.

To Don's surprise, Walter Wallace laughed. "So they

hit you up for the old so-called voluntary contribution, did they? Well, it was just a matter of time. How much is it this year?"

"Four percent."

"No worse than last campaign. I thought they might up it a little after Joe Tittle lost his councilman's seat."

Don stared at him. "You know about this . . . this macing?" He'd picked up the word from Gil.

Wallace shrugged. "It's gone on for years, Don. It's just the dues for working for the city."

"That's what Gil Barber called it."

"Barber?"

"One of the guys in the drafting room."

"He sounds pretty savvy."

"Am I wrong," Don said carefully, "or do I get the idea that you think this asking for a kickback is all right?"

Mrs. Wallace laughed nervously. "Now come on, you two. This is supposed to be a cookout, not a political forum. Your hamburgers are getting cold."

"Mr. Wall—Walter, I'd like to know just where you stand," Don persisted.

"Is that a challenge, young fellow?"

"No, it's just a request for information."

Sue's voice cut in, a trifle high-pitched. "Don—"

"It's all right," Wallace said with a little wave of his hand. "Look, Don, when you took that city job, you must have realized that it was a political appointment. I got our councilman, Hailey Hanover, to sign your application. He's a close friend of mine, and he was glad to do it, but that still makes your job a political one."

"I earn every dollar I get paid." Don put down his plate. He suddenly had no taste for food.

"I know you do. Most of you do. If all city employees sat on their cans—"

"Walter!"

"Sorry, Elizabeth. I'm just pointing out that the fact Don works hard at his job doesn't make it any less of a political appointment. And political appointees in this city have always been expected to support the party."

"And you think that's the way things should continue to be?"

"Let me put it this way, Don. That's the way things have been done ever since I can remember, and it's a system that seems to work. This is a well-run city. It's not going bankrupt like New York, and it's not falling apart physically like a lot of other cities I could name. So don't be so quick to condemn the way it operates."

Don slammed the flat of his hand on his snack table. His plate and silver clattered. "But it's *crooked!* Taking money from employees is crooked!"

"Not if it's voluntary."

"But it *isn't* voluntary—not the way it's been explained to me."

"I've never heard of anyone being fired because he wouldn't contribute."

"You don't think they're going to make an announcement in the papers, do you?"

"Now, Don," Elizabeth Wallace cautioned.

"I'm sorry, Mrs. Wallace, but I—"

"It's Elizabeth, dear."

"I'm not trying to start an argument. I'm just getting tired of everybody saying that something is really okay when I know darned well it's wrong. And that isn't changed just because it has been done that way for a long time. Doesn't anyone care about honesty anymore?"

"You're talking like a Boy Scout," Wallace shot back. "This is real life, the way things operate. A little oil here, a little grease there, and the world keeps moving. You understand what I'm saying?"

"Sure, I understand. What you're saying is that a crooked arrangement should be kept alive because everybody's geared to do business that way. I'll tell you one thing, though. *Everybody* hasn't gotten used to it. I haven't."

Wallace carefully set down his iced-tea glass. "Are you trying to tell us that you don't intend to turn in your share of the Department of Streets contribution?"

Faced with the direct question, Don discovered that he didn't have a direct answer. "I'm . . . still deciding." He wanted to kick himself. What had happened to all the big talk between him and Hobie? Where was his courage when he really could use some?"

"Fair enough," Wallace said agreeably, "so long as you ultimately decide to do the right thing. Let me give you a little piece of free advice, though. And I'm talking as a lawyer as well as your father-in-law. Don't go around broadcasting your thoughts about the morality of all this. You never know who could be listening, and like all cities, this one is highly political."

He reached for the pitcher and poured himself another glass of frosty tea. "There's another point. Just among the four of us. I may decide to run for City Council one of these fine days—"

"Walter!" Mrs. Wallace burst out. "How wonderful!"

He silenced her with an impatient gesture. "My point is that if the word got around that I couldn't even keep my own son-in-law in line, I might have a bit of a time getting the backing of the party organization."

He lifted his glass in a salute. "I hadn't meant to get so serious. After all, this is supposed to be a family get-together. I'll offer a toast to you two kids. Congratulations on your first six months of marriage."

"Some supper!" Don growled as he drove the old Ford back to the Timberlane Apartments.

Sue had won the bet. Her father had advised Don to go along with the contribution, but she was silent.

"I'm getting sick of everybody telling me that I shouldn't rock the canoe just because it has always been paddled the same old corrupt way," he muttered. He looked over at her in the glow of the dash lights. "Sue?"

"What?"

"You, too? You're giving me the silent treatment because I don't want to kick back *our* money?"

"No. Not because of the money. Because you argued with my father and upset my mother. And me."

"I'm sorry it turned out the way it did, hon. But you can't want me just to say whatever is going to make your dad happy. I happen to disagree with him on this kickback thing because I think he's wrong."

"It didn't have to turn into such a big argument."

"I didn't know it would come out that way."

"You could have been able to guess, since he did get your job application signed for you. You should have realized that he's involved with the party himself."

"I should have? I should have? What's going on? You're the one who insisted that I ask him about it. Next thing I know, everybody's sniping at me. Now I see how the kickback thing goes on and on. Nobody's got guts enough to blow the whistle."

"Or is dumb enough."

29

He stared at her. "Is that how I look to you? Now my own wife has become part of the system!"

"I was only trying to . . ." She turned away.

They drove in silence for three long blocks. "Look," he forced himself to say, "let's not let a stupid thing like this get us mad at each other."

"I'm not mad," Sue said softly. "It's just that you got Daddy and Mother upset when I thought we'd all have such a nice evening together."

He pounded the heel of his hand on the steering wheel. "I don't understand anything about this! You want me not to question something I know is crooked just so we can keep peace in the family? Is that all my honesty means to you?"

"Oh, honesty! You keep harping on that like somebody's asking you to rob a bank. It's only a donation, Don."

"It's two hundred and sixty dollars of protection money to keep my job."

"You don't know that. It's only what Gil and some of the others have told you. Do you really know of anybody being fired because he refused to make the donation?"

She had a neat but maddening way of backing him into corners.

"No," he was forced to admit.

"Then all this threat stuff could be in your own head."

He slowed for a yellow light that held long enough for them to slip through. "No, it's not in my head. The little talk I had with Charlie Pegler wasn't in my head. Neither was that talk with your father tonight. If you think I'm exaggerating this whole thing, why don't I march in there Monday and tell them they aren't going to get a dime out of us?"

"You can't do that!"

"Why not? You think I've blown this all out of shape. Suppose there really isn't anything to it after all? Why not test them?"

"Because," she said slowly, "you will embarrass Daddy."

"Oh, great! I'm to fork over two hundred and sixty bucks to keep from embarrassing Daddy. Where's your head, Sue?"

She whirled back to the window, and he knew from the set of her shoulders that he was in for a long, cold night with the silent treatment probably going right into the next day. Some weekend.

All right, if that was the way she wanted it. Tomorrow he'd be a good party hack. He would put up the posters. Alone. That would take care of at least half of Saturday.

CHAPTER 5

WARREN ROAD where it crossed Country Boulevard was empty when Don pulled to the shoulder around nine. He switched off the ignition, picked up his hammer, the box of tacks, and one of the red-white-and-blue SID HARTE, YOUR CHOICE FOR CITY COUNCIL posters.

He slid out of the seat and trotted across the pavement to a power pole in the safety island in the middle of Country Boulevard. The morning sun was bright and the cloudless day promised to be pleasantly warm. There was no traffic yet. He was glad of that. He didn't want to be seen doing this. He was a highway draftsman, not a lousy ward heeler! But he'd promised Charlie Pegler he would go through with it.

He fumbled with the hammer and got the first tack in sideways. That was okay with him. Let the poster blow away after he'd left. He didn't care.

He heard a car pull out of Warren Road and stop

behind him. He looked over his shoulder at a blue-and-white Millbury Police cruiser.

"Hey, fella," the chunky officer at the wheel called, "don't you know it's illegal to put posters on poles?"

Oh, fine.

"Yes," Don called back. He stood there with his hammer aimed at the second tack, not sure of his next move.

"Wise kid," the officer grumbled to his partner. "Who you working for, kid?"

"Sid Harte." The morning wasn't yet hot, but perspiration was beginning to run into Don's eyes.

The cop's change of pace was remarkable. "Oh. Why didn't you say so? Look, kid, don't be so obvious about putting those up, will you? Put 'em on trees where nobody's going to give you a hard time. We can't run escort for you." The engine surged, and the police car rolled away down Country Boulevard.

"Don't you know it's illegal to put posters on trees, too?" Don muttered to himself. "Say the magic words, *Sid Harte,* and make friends with the police while you're breaking the law." He picked up his tack box and walked back to the Ford.

He hung Sid Harte on maples, beeches, and oaks from Warren Road to Greenvale Lane, then drove back into town feeling that he'd just sold part of himself dirt cheap, just as Gil had told him . . . as he himself told Sue when he got home.

"That's a silly way to look at it." She had come out of her cold silence when he arrived with two Monsterburgers from Carloff's Drive-In. She can be bought for a hamburger, he thought. But he didn't say it.

"It's not so silly. I felt like a scruffy ward heeler out

there, nailing up junk posters for the big boss. It made me one of the boys, all right. The police even looked the other way. Wonder what they would have done if those had been posters for the opposition? I'd probably be calling your father for bail money."

Sue put down her Monsterburger, stood up, and walked around the kitchen table. "On your feet."

"What?"

"On your feet, dimwit."

He stood, shaking his head. He noticed that clean soap smell again that always made him weak. "I don't see—"

"You don't see a lot. Put your arms around me. That's right. Now kiss me."

He pecked her lightly. He wasn't going to give in easily.

"Call that a kiss? *This* is a kiss."

He whistled as he came up for air, his nerve ends tingling. "Look, sweet Sue, don't kiss like that unless you're looking for trouble."

"I wouldn't mind."

With that, the phone rang.

Don sighed as he reached for the receiver.

"Don, this is Hobie."

"Your timing is fantastic."

"Just got something over the wire you might find interesting, ol' buddy. There's been a federal indictment in New Jersey of a Welfare Department official. Seems he was forcing his employees to ante up a little election money. What do you think of them apples?"

"Makes me wish Millbury were in New Jersey."

"Don't you see? If we put out the word here, the same thing could happen. Isn't that what you want?"

"A federal indictment of Charlie Pegler?"

There was a pause. Then Hobie said, "Is that who's putting the pressure on you?"

"I didn't say that. What are you trying to do to me?"

"Make a hero out of you."

"Make a victim out of me, you mean. Anything for a story! Wow, cool off that typewriter, will you? I spent the morning nailing up posters for good old Sid Harte. Does that sound like a renegade from the party?"

He could hear Hobie tapping something on something. He rolled his eyes at Sue, and she rolled hers back at him. Talking politics was the last thing either of them wanted to do on this particular lazy afternoon.

"Sounds like all your fire has turned to fizzle," Hobie said. His voice held a little undertone of something Don didn't like.

"I guess it does sound that way," Don said. "I don't know where I do stand, to be truthful about it. I thought I did. Then Sue's father jumped all over me—"

"What did you expect? He's a solid party man, right down the line."

"If I weren't married, I wouldn't be so—" He could have kicked himself for hiding behind Sue.

"Ol' buddy," Hobie persisted, "they're going to own you if you let them. Take my word for it. You do it my way, and you'll keep your self-respect."

"Yeah, but that's something we can't live on for very long."

"And it's something you won't like much to live without, Don. Keep in touch. I think you're going to need me."

Don replaced the phone. "That was a dirty trick. Hobie's got my stomach in a granny knot." He sat down with a frown. Sue ran her fingers through his hair.

"I'm good at untying knots, hon. Let's forget about

all this. Let's just think about us for the rest of the day."

"All this *is* about us, Sue."

"You know what I mean."

He reached out and pulled her into his lap. "If I only knew enough about street design, we could be on our way out of Millbury right now. Money in the bank. The big job waiting. But it's going to take those eighteen months more."

"Don't talk so much." She held his face between her hands and kissed him gently.

"You're right. Talking time is over."

What was left of their Monsterburgers began to grow cold, but they didn't care.

The phone rang in pitch-darkness. Don fought out of the fuzz of sleep and pulled his arm out from under Sue.

She woke up with a little jump. "What? What is it, hon?"

"Phone. At one in the morning."

He stumbled into the kitchen and grabbed for the receiver on the fourth ring.

"Ellison?"

"Yes." His heart pounded. You got calls at this time of night only if your dad or mom was— He didn't recognize the man's voice.

"Sorry to be calling so late, Ellison. Just got in from a meeting. Your name came up."

"What meeting? What are you talking about?"

"Party organizational get-together. We're tying up loose ends. You're not going to be one of them, are you, Ellison?" The man's voice was raspy and purposeful.

"I don't know what you mean."

"You know exactly what I mean. The Man Downstairs wants one hundred percent cooperation, and you've been mouthing around about not giving it. He don't appreciate it, Ellison. I'm doing you a favor telling you that. The party don't stand for city workers that aren't loyal. You follow me?"

"Who is this?" Don demanded.

"A friend, friend. We want you to simmer down and be a good boy. You get the message?" The connection clicked off.

Don couldn't place the heavy voice at all. He went back to the bedroom and sat on the edge of the bed with sweat chilling his shoulders.

Sue knelt beside him. "Who was it, hon?"

"That's just it. I don't know."

"I was afraid it was your mom or dad calling from Clairmont. You know . . . this time of night." With her fingertips, she turned his face toward her. "Don?"

"I've never gotten an anonymous call before. Sure shakes you up." The guy had referred to The Man Downstairs. That could make him a Department of Streets employee assigned to ask Don to— Ask? You don't call at one in the morning to ask. That had been a call carefully timed to scare him. It had worked, too. He sat there shivering.

"Come to bed, hon." She tried to sound casual, but her voice gave her away. She lay down and moved close beside him, hoping the warmth of her body would drive out the chill. But his feeling of dread wouldn't go away, and Sue sensed it.

"You're sure you don't know who it was?"

"I've never heard that voice before. It was a man maybe in his fifties. Kind of gravelly."

37

His arms tightened around her. Somewhere in Millbury, unknown people had tossed his name around; then one of them had wakened him with a threatening phone call. That was enough to shake you up.

And it could make you mad, too, he began to realize. Who were they to invade his and Sue's life like this?

"Dammit!" he said in the darkness. He sat up and threw the sheet aside.

"Don!"

"I'm going to call Hobie."

"At this time of night?"

"He won't care."

Don was right. "You can wake me up anytime at all, ol' buddy, with this kind of call. You got any idea who woke you up?"

"Not a clue. But it's the last straw, Hobie. I'm scared, but I'm mad, too. And I'm more mad than I'm scared. If this is how Millbury is run, I want to do what I can to change it."

"Now you're talking! I'm going to write a story that will break things wide open."

"Wait a minute. It's not that easy. There are some people I don't want to hurt."

There was silence at the other end of the line. Then Hobie said, "Sometimes a newspaper story is like a shotgun, Don. You can aim it at the bull's-eye, but it's liable to hit all over the place. You've got to make up your mind. Either you go all out, or you don't go at all."

"It's not a black or white thing. I don't want to hurt Sue or her parents or Charlie Pegler."

"Or yourself?"

"I guess you could say that."

"Then you don't want me to write a story."

"Come on, Hobie. The trouble with you is that you want to write the big one or nothing. There's got to be a way to nail a couple of crooks without flattening everybody who's within earshot of the hammer."

"Hold it a sec. The water just boiled. I'm getting a cup of coffee." Hobie was back in less than a minute. "That's better. Listen, I've got an idea. I'll make you an authoritative source."

"Anonymous quotes?"

"I'll admit it's not the strongest way to go, but it'll be a start."

"That's good enough for me. They just used an anonymous phone call on me. We'll use anonymous quotes on them. When will the story run?"

"Monday morning. But I'd better warn you, ol' buddy. It won't be the end of anything. It'll be just the beginning."

CHAPTER 6

DON COULD FEEL the tension in the drafting room as he reached the top of the stairs on Monday morning.

Gil didn't waste the time to say good morning. "Did you see it? Did you see that story in the paper?" His voice was low, and his eyes darted toward Charlie Pegler's office as if he were afraid some sort of lightning would flash out of the glassed-in cubicle. In there, Pegler and Marty Corrigan stood hunched over Pegler's reference table.

"I saw the article," Don said. "What are they up to in there?"

"They're reading it in Pegler's copy of the *Chronicle*. This whole place is in an uproar over who's blabbing to the press."

Don pulled the cover off his drafting table and began to fold it. The air-conditioning started up, and its chill made him shiver. Or was it more than the cool air?

"Who do you think?" Gil blurted.

"Who do I think what?"

"Gave out that scoop to the paper on the kickback?"

"I thought you considered it a voluntary contribution, like The Man Downstairs said, Gil."

"That isn't what the *Chronicle* calls it. Who could have given out that story? Charlie Pegler? He's never liked the system much."

Don's mouth went dry. "Could have been anybody." He hadn't expected the newspaper story to have such a sudden and close-to-home effect. True, it had been on page one of the *Millbury Chronicle,* but not in the headlines. The four-paragraph piece had been at the bottom of the page in a little box.

"Could have been old Al Hill," Gil persisted, "except he's so close to retirement. Or maybe Kent Watters . . . or Eddie Koslowski. Or even a couple of others who grit their teeth when that contribution memo comes around." Gil grinned slyly and added, "Or it could have been me. What do you think of that?"

You're ready to jump aboard the winning wagon, Don thought, no matter where it's headed. "Was it you?" he asked. He was irritated by Gil's know-it-all attitude. Would Gil actually take credit for something he had no part of?

"If I didn't know you so well, I'd ask you the same question, Don, buddy."

Don stuck his drafting pencil into the point sander and turned it slowly. "You said you thought it might be Al Hill or Kent Watters or Eddie Koslowski. I thought I was the only frustrated rebel in here."

"Nope. There's a group of us."

"Us?"

"Sure. You're included."

That wasn't what Don meant. He had been surprised that Gil included himself.

"We're ready to bolt if we can only get it together," Gil went on, his voice low. "That newspaper story might be the start of something interesting."

Don studied Gil's face. The redheaded ex-Navy man sure was a hard guy to read. A couple days ago, he had been pumping out the party line to shut up and pay. Now he seemed to be swinging the other way. Which was the real Gil?

Hill, Watters, and Koslowski. And maybe others? That was interesting. Don had thought that he was way out on a lonely limb. Now it looked as if he had some company.

At nine fifteen, Charlie Pegler got a phone call and scurried downstairs. Twenty minutes later he reappeared, looking as if he'd wrestled a bear. His face was red, his hair was rumpled, and his mouth was set in a hard line. He caught Al Hill's eye and jerked his thumb toward his glass cubicle.

Old Al laid down his pencil, took off his steel-rimmed glasses, dropped them in his vest pocket, and clumped to Pegler's office. Nearby, Billy Crimm looked up, then back down quickly, as if he didn't want anyone to realize he'd noticed anything.

Pegler shut the door. His mouth moved and his arms waved, but Don and Gil couldn't hear a thing through the distant glass.

"Sure looks like old Al's getting an earful," Gil said.

Pegler went on for a full minute, then asked Al a question. Al shrugged. Pegler let loose another mouthful. Al shrugged again.

Pegler yanked open the door, and Al ambled back to

his chair by the corner window, his eyes fixed straight ahead.

"Looked like he just stood there and took whatever Charlie was handing out," Don said.

"If you had only a little while to hold on until retirement, what would you do? Al's playing it careful. He hears nothing, sees nothing, says nothing."

"You just said you thought he might be the one who talked to the press, Gil."

"Ah, you forget the senility factor. Old men have strange ways."

The next to get the signal from Charlie Pegler was Kent Watters, a tall, spidery fellow addicted to wild sports shirts. With a quick jerk of his head, he twitched back his earlobe-length black hair and walked through the rows of drafting tables with a sidewise scuttle.

"Guess Kent opened his mouth once too often," Gil said. "Pegler's working his way down the dog list."

Behind the glass, Pegler stared at Kent Watters sourly; then his words appeared to tumble out like machine-gun fire.

A band of bright red arose from Watters' purple shirt collar. He snapped out about five words. Pegler rapped back at him. Kent twisted his thin lips, then shook his head.

"Al Hill says nothing. Kent says no," Gil interpreted. "Any bets on who's next?"

They both were sure it would be Eddie Koslowski. They were right. Eddie's eyebrows shot up, and he walked to the office wearing a perplexed frown. He was a heavy-set middle-aged man who always wore his sleeves rolled up and his tie pulled down. He ran his fingers through his thinning wheat-colored hair and closed Pegler's office door behind him.

43

Charlie Pegler went through the same angry routine. Eddie's wide mouth twisted into something close to a wry grin. He said something that made Charlie shake his head and do an Al Hill shrug himself. He waved Eddie away and turned toward the drafting room. His eyes fastened on Don.

"Oh, Lord," Don moaned.

Pegler pointed straight at him and jerked his head.

"Congratulations!" Gil muttered, his head down. "You've made the dog list."

Don walked to Pegler's glass cage on rubbery legs. "Shut the door," Pegler commanded. "You know why you're here?"

"I'm not sure," Don said carefully. "There are some rumors going around out there." He let his eyes move past Charlie Pegler into the drafting room. Every face seemed to be staring at him.

Pegler pointed at the copy of the *Chronicle* on his table. "Seen that?"

"Yes, I have."

"What do you think of it?"

"It's accurate."

"I don't mean that." Pegler's gray forelock jiggled. "What do you think of anybody who would give out that information?"

That was a nice rattrap of a question. "I think," Don said slowly, wishing he weren't beginning to sweat beneath his shirt, "I think if something can't be made public, then it shouldn't be done in the first place."

Pegler looked confused. "Haven't you ever heard of corporate secrets? A company can't just blab everything to the public."

"But this is a city agency. Don't the taxpayers have a right to know whatever goes on?"

44

After a long pause, Pegler said, "I think they have a right to see the results of their investment. The streets in this city are as good as any, better than most." His expression tightened. "Dammit! That's not the point! The Man Downstairs has hit the ceiling over this thing in the paper this morning. He wants to know who talked to that reporter, and he's asked me to help him find out."

"So he thinks somebody up here did it."

"He suspects. But he's checking downstairs, too."

Don took a chance. "Why doesn't he call the reporter?"

"He did. The guy wouldn't tell him a thing."

Thank Heavens Hobie was living up to his promise to keep Don's name out of it.

"So I'm the upstairs detective," Pegler went on. "Not because I want to be, but I'm going to do as I'm told. Can't afford it any other way. Now level with me, Don. Was it you?"

He wouldn't lie. He had to divert. "Are you going through the whole department, man by man?"

"If I have to. But I'm starting with the most likely ones."

"The dog list, Gil calls it."

Pegler frowned. "Well, there's no list. I'm pretty good at identifying potential troublemakers without a computer readout."

"And you've got me pegged as a troublemaker."

"I hope not. But I'm covering all the bases."

"In this goldfish bowl."

Pegler nodded. "I want to be obvious about it." He slapped the newspaper. "Maybe it'll discourage this kind of problem in the future. All right, get out of here. We've held up that Conklin Street job long enough."

Don returned to his drafting table. "Al shrugged it off," Gil said. "Kent said no. Eddie joked it away. I'd say you debated it to death. Pegler's after the stoolie, like we thought, right?"

"If you want to put it that way."

"Is there another way?"

"I thought you were all for the guy who gave out the story. You change sides faster than a hockey puck."

Gil frowned. "I might agree with what he did, but I have to say the guy is a stool pigeon. He gave out a story on confidential information, didn't he? What else can you call him?"

"You could consider him something of a watchdog for the public. And nothing on that memo said it was confidential, by the way."

Gil studied him for long silent seconds. "You know something? I'm beginning to think you're the guy!"

Don hoped nothing showed in his face. "Call out those stadia shots," he said. "Here comes Corrigan."

Most of the draftsmen brought their lunches. The brown-bag brigade lounged on the rear lawn between the building and the parking lot with their home-brought sandwiches and soft drinks from the machine just inside the rear door. Afterward, they were careful to pick up every scrap of paper and deposit it in the green-and-white trash barrels at the corners of the parking lot. Once someone had left a square of paper in the middle of the lawn during lunchtime. In the early afternoon, The Man Downstairs had ordered Pegler to send down everyone who had eaten lunch outside. He hadn't come out himself, but Don had seen him watching from his corner office window while Marty

Corrigan tore the waxed paper into seventeen pieces, one for each of them to carry to the trash barrels. The fact that nobody had protested this mass disciplining showed you how tight jobs were in Millbury, Don had told Sue.

That had been the only time he'd actually seen The Man Downstairs, just that massive head silhouetted in the corner window. Yet the Department of Streets director controlled a good part of his life, as he controlled much of the life of every employee in the department.

Don and Gil squatted on the cool grass well away from that powerful corner window. Nobody but an occasional new employee ate his lunch over there, and he soon moved to the other side of the lawn after he was put wise.

Don unwrapped his peanut-butter-and-jelly on whole wheat.

"Ellison?" Kent Watters stood over him, twitching his long hair out of his face. "Can I talk to you a minute?"

"Sure, Kent. Sit down."

"I mean alone." Kent looked at Gil.

"Well, excuse *me!* I wanted to get another grape soda anyway." Gil got to his feet and walked away toward the building. Kent sat on his heels.

"Eddie Koslowski says to tell you that he and I are with you," he said, with a quick glance toward the distant corner office.

"What do you mean, you're with me?"

"You know what I mean. We're not going to stand for the kind of pushing around we got from Pegler this morning, are we?"

"There isn't a heck of a lot we can do about it, is there? Outside of quitting. I don't think any of us is in a position to do that. I sure know I'm not."

"There's one thing we can do that will really hit them. We can refuse to pay the kickback they're asking for."

Don took a bite of his sandwich. "Why are you telling me all this? I'm practically new around here."

"Because you seem to be the kind of guy with the guts to stand up for what he knows is right."

"Is that what Eddie thinks, too?"

"That's what he told me. We've been waiting for somebody like you to come along."

"What about Al Hill? He was in there with Pegler this morning, like the rest of us."

"Al's too close to retirement. He mutters around about the system, they pick him up on it, then he backs down and behaves. It's just his way of letting off steam after twenty-nine years of this stuff."

"What about Gil?"

"I'm not sure I trust Gil. You didn't see him in there this morning, did you?"

"I didn't see a lot of guys in there, Kent, but I hope there are a few more besides you, Eddie, and me who don't like the setup."

Kent ran his fingers through his hair. "Nobody likes the setup, but only a few of us are willing to speak up about it."

"Speak up? I didn't know anybody had said anything."

"The word's around that you put that story in the paper this morning."

Don looked at Kent's half-smile. He felt sweat popping out on his forehead. The sandwich was suddenly tasteless. He fought to keep his voice steady.

"What gave you the idea—"

"Come on, Don. You're the only one of us who knows that reporter."

"Who says?"

"Gil says."

Good old Gil. "You believe what he tells you?"

"In this case, it's good enough for Eddie and me. Listen, Don, we're with you. We don't want to pay up any more than you do."

"I can't afford it. Even with Sue working."

Kent thumped him on the shoulder. "Atta boy! It's not just Eddie and me. There'll be more. You'll see."

He rose in one easy motion and walked back toward the parking area, where Eddie Koslowski was making some adjustment under the hood of his car. If The Man Downstairs is watching, Don realized, Kent has just linked all of us together like a big iron chain.

CHAPTER 7

THE CITY POLICE cruiser had followed
them for three blocks. Suddenly its
lights flashed red and blue. The cruiser pulled alongside; its driver mo-
tioned Don to the curb, then angled in ahead of him.
The officer was sapling thin at first glance but turned
out to be a shade flabby around the middle. He was like
a whippet settling into an easy life.

"Your license, Ellison."

Don reached for his wallet, surprised that the officer
already knew his name.

"Take it out of the wallet and hand it to me."

"What's the problem? I was only doing thirty."

"That's right, Ellison. But your license plate looks
like you dipped it in chocolate pudding. Law says it's
got to be readable."

"I'll clean it off as soon as we get home," Don said
with relief. Talk about a nothing kind of a charge!

"No good. Get out and clean it off now."

"You're kidding!"

"Try me."

Sue laid her hand on Don's arm. "He means it, honey. Please do what he says."

Don had to use his clean handkerchief, and it was a grimy rag when he finished. He got back in the car tight-lipped and silent.

"See you keep it clean in the future, Ellison. And watch yourself in this town." The cruiser roared away.

"I didn't know the police stopped people for dumb things like a muddy license plate." Sue's voice was small and scared. He knew that she sensed there was more to this than one over-eager police officer.

"I've never heard of it happening even once." He twisted the ignition key. "Let's go home."

Watch yourself in this town, the cop had warned him. The thing would have been nothing more than a trivial incident, except for that.

Just after eleven that same night, the phone blasted the apartment's stillness.

"Now what?" Don muttered. He hated to leave the coziness of the bed. "Someday I hope we can afford more than one phone. Or else let's have that one moved in here, or the bed out there."

The thing kept jangling. He got up and stumbled over the corner of the bed in the darkness. "I'm coming. I'm coming."

"Ellison?"

Before his name was half said, Don realized this was his gravel-voiced caller of a few nights ago.

"You again." He managed to keep his voice steady, but his stomach began to knot.

"You didn't listen the last time, Ellison. I asked you to

fall in line, and instead you went and got a jerk newspaper reporter all excited over nothing."

The receiver was wet in Don's palm.

"It's not hard to figure out, Ellison. Millbury isn't all that big a city. You follow me?" The caller paused, as if he were drinking or eating something. Don fought an impulse to hang up. But that wouldn't accomplish anything. The guy simply would ring back, ring and ring until Don answered again . . . or left the phone off the hook. Maybe that would—

"Listen, Ellison. We're disappointed in you. Know what I mean? We asked you in a reasonable way to toe the line, and you go shoot off your mouth to the newspapers. But I'll show you how reasonable we still are. You shut your mouth up tight from here on in, pay up, and you won't have any more problems. You follow me?"

Don was silent.

"Ellison?"

"Aren't you allowed to tell me who you are?"

"We're talking about you, Ellison, not me. You pay attention to what I've said, you understand?"

"I understand what you're saying, all right."

"Good. That's real good. But I don't think you're really convinced yet. I think you're a know-it-all kid. You'll find out what happens to know-it-all kids, Ellison. Just make sure you keep your license plate clean." He laughed and hung up in the middle of it.

In a fury Don leaned against the cool porcelain of the refrigerator. Was this going to go on night after night?

"Who was it, hon?" Sue called from the bedroom darkness.

"Old gravel voice again. Telling me to keep my license plate clean."

She clicked on the bed lamp as he sat on the bed. Her face was pale. "He knew about that?"

"Maybe he's . . ." It was almost too monstrous to say. "Maybe he's a cop. Cops work for the city, too. Just like us streets and highways folks. We're all one big corrupt family."

At midnight, thirteen miles across Millbury, a stocky man in his late fifties relaxed in his pine-paneled study and lit his second cigar of the evening. Each pull on it flattened his slab-sided cheeks, and his long forehead was wrinkled with concentration.

He was bald with only a gray horseshoe around the back of his long head, yet he looked much younger than his age. That was because of his eyes. They were wide-set, icy blue. When they locked on you, they were hawk's eyes. They never seemed to blink. They drilled much deeper than you liked.

It was not this man's face that had propelled him to political power. The face sloped forward like a plow into a great chin that hid his short neck. The lips were pale, and he appeared to have just a tight slash for a mouth. His nose was puffy and shapeless. Only the eyes were alive in that face.

What had gotten this man the power he had—and he had a lot—was his ability to use one person against another. That had put Carleton J. Munroe, The Man Downstairs, where he was this warm July midnight. And he was somewhere.

Munroe was a Millbury political boss. In fact, he was *the* Millbury political boss. Several of the other department heads—Len Rhodes of Sanitation, Ernie Kupke, who headed Water Services, Glen Stone, the police chief—had some political clout. But they were newcomers to the political scene just gaining a degree of power under Mayor Arch Norwall. Munroe had ridden upward through three administrations, managing to survive even when the party he backed first went down the drain of defeat. He did it by keeping a heavy finger in both parties' maneuverings at state level, making the switch when he had to.

He took the cigar from his thin, whitish lips, looked down at its coal, then up at the man who sat across from him in the small room.

"I appreciate your coming out here tonight, Billy. You sure you don't want one of these?"

"Nope. Don't smoke."

"Um," Munroe said. Billy Crimm probably didn't drink, either. He just came whenever you called and did whatever you asked him to do. That was why Munroe kept Billy Crimm on at the Department of Streets. Crimm was a lousy engineer but a terrific spy. He was big and rapidly going to paunch, but he still had heavy black hair. Combed straight back, it gave his head the look of an artillery shell.

"So you think it's— Who did you say?" Munroe decided to play ignorant for the moment.

"Kid named Ellison."

"One of the new draftsmen."

"Came on at the beginning of the year," Crimm said.

"Why do you think he's the one who talked to the newspapers?"

"Little things add up. Feeling I got. Feeling you get when you've been in that drafting room long enough."

Crimm hardly ever spoke in complete sentences. That irritated Munroe, but he tried hard not to show it. Planting your own one-hundred-percent-loyal man in

Charlie Pegler's drafting room hadn't been easy. Munroe could put up with a lot of irritation to keep him there.

"That's enough for you to go on?" Munroe asked.

"Don't have to go on it. Just the way I feel. You have to decide yourself." Crimm always managed to suggest more than he actually said.

"I'll take your word for it. Already have." Crimm's partial sentences were contagious. Munroe always made an effort to keep his grammar neat. He'd never gone to college. He had come up the hard way, and he tried to speak flawlessly to hide that fact.

"You mean you sent word to Glen Stone," Crimm said, his eyes steady on Munroe's.

How had Crimm known that? "Well, as a matter of fact, yes. I told him to put a little heat on the boy. Just a touch, though. After all, young Ellison had his application signed by Hailey Hanover." He watched Crimm's face. A few minutes ago, he'd purposely sounded hazy about Ellison. Now he had hit Crimm with the fact that he'd already done some digging on his own. That was how you had to play it with these people: stay two jumps ahead of them all the time and be sure you let them know it.

Crimm made an effort to recover lost one-upmanship. "Hanover didn't sign it because he knew Ellison, though."

"I know that. Walt Wallace was the contact—Ellison's father-in-law. But however it came about, the boy has Hanover's name on his application."

"And Wallace as his father-in-law."

"Therefore, I don't want to step on any more toes than I have to." Why couldn't the rebel in his Department of Streets have been somebody with a nobody for a father-in-law and another councilman's name on his job application? Hailey Hanover had once said that political bosses were dinosaurs, that they should decently fade into the sunset and let the business of city and state go on without all their backstage string pulling. And Walt Wallace, so rumor had it, was thinking of running for city council himself. Fine pickle if he made it, then came after Carleton J. Munroe for dumping his son-in-law!

The Man Downstairs fixed his gaze on the thread of smoke climbing from his cigar. This problem had him thinking hard. He didn't want to cross swords with Councilman Hanover or with Walter Wallace. He wondered if Ellison realized just what he had going for himself.

"Maybe Glen Stone's boys in blue will throw some sense into Ellison," Crimm said. "Give him such a hard time he'll pack and run."

"Out of Millbury, I hope. Then that'll be the end of it. We can't afford to let even one fellow buck the system and get away with it. The whole structure is too delicate. It works, but it's vulnerable to a lot of things." Such as blind honesty, he thought. "That's why we have to stop revolts before they start."

"With fast action," Crimm offered with a half-smile.

"To be more specific," Munroe answered, still studying his cigar, "with fear."

CHAPTER 8

THE CALL-DIRECTOR panel flashed. Sue punched the button. "Castleton Printing. Good afternoon."

"Mrs. Ellison, please. Mrs. Donald Ellison." The voice was odd, like the voice of a radio announcer who was trying to keep his tones deep but needed to clear his throat.

Sue frowned. She never got calls of her own here at the lobby switchboard unless it was Don telling her he'd be late picking her up after work. But this certainly wasn't Don's voice. The man sounded brisk and official.

"This is Mrs. Ellison."

"Millbury Police, Mrs. Ellison. Sorry to have to tell you this, but we understand there's been an accident. Your husband—"

A numbness raced along her back. Her fingers trembled on the call-director buttons. She had a wild impulse to push them all and scream for help.

"Mrs. Ellison?"

She forced herself to concentrate. "Is he—"

"No details yet. I'll have to call you back." The connection was broken.

She had to get out of here! She punched 214.

"Art Josky."

"Mr. Josky, I have to leave. I've got to! It's Don. There's been an accident—"

Josky, the office manager, had been an Army medic before he began his career with Castleton. He knew hysteria when he heard it. "Sue, is that you? Sit tight. I'll be right out."

He trotted out of his office past a secretary's desk. "Marcie, we've got a problem. Spell Sue at the front desk, will you? What you're doing can wait."

The little brunette had to run to keep up with her storklike boss. In the lobby, she took everything in with a glance. Sue was in tears, her face gray. Her shoulders shook, but she was still trying to handle incoming calls.

"Take a break, honey," Marcie said, smoothly lifting the mini-mike and earplug from Sue's head and fitting them to her head. "Good afternoon. Castleton Printing."

Marcie noticed with amazement that old Josky had his arm around Sue and was leading her back to his office. Who would have expected such tenderness from Big Bird, as they all called the gangling office manager behind his back? And what in the world had happened to Sue?

Josky wondered the same thing as he drew a cup of coffee from the drip machine in the corner of his office.

"Now don't talk yet. Take a sip or two; then let's see if I can be of any help."

She did as she was told, gulping the coffee like a child. Then her words burst out shrill and scared.

"The police. They called. Don's been in an accident. I've got to go, Mr. Josky. I've got to go!"

"Where is he?"

She looked at him blankly. "They said—" Her eyes searched his. "Where is he? They didn't tell me. They didn't tell me!"

Odd, Josky thought. "Just sit tight a minute." He patted her arm and lifted his phone receiver.

The sergeant on duty seemed mystified. "We got no report on any Ellison here."

"And all such calls would have come through you?"

"Yes, sir. You sure you got the right name?"

Josky hung up, puzzled. "Maybe good news, Sue. They don't seem to know anything about it." He rubbed his chin. "If I remember correctly, your husband works at the Department of Streets."

Sue nodded. She was afraid to hope and afraid not to. The coffee cup jiggled in her fingers as she drew a long, shuddering breath.

Josky punched his touch-tone buttons with a long forefinger. "You have a Don Ellison there? I'd like to speak to him, please." A long pause, then his face brightened and he held the phone out to Sue.

"Don? *Don!* Oh, darling, they said you were—" The tears came, hot and uncontrollable. Josky took the phone from her shaking fingers.

"Mr. Ellison, this is Art Josky, office manager at Castleton. I'm afraid your wife has been the victim of a hoax—a damned cruel one. I'm sure she'll be all right shortly, but I'm inclined to give her the rest of the day off if you can get yourself free to come pick her up. She's in no condition to be alone."

"There's no way they could keep me here," Don said.

Good man, Josky commended him silently. He'd never met Ellison, but his wife was tops. She came from a well-to-do-family, he understood, but did a fine job at whatever she was assigned.

He replaced the receiver. "A hoax, Sue. Some people get their kicks that way. They're sick, but that's no reason for you to be. Don is on his way to take you home. We'll see you tomorrow, okay?"

She managed a thin smile. "I think so, Mr. Josky."

The office manager smiled back. He was a peaceful man, but at this moment he could cheerfully bludgeon whoever had sent his receptionist into such a tailspin.

Sue felt an overpowering need to sit close against Don in the car, to clutch his arm with both hands as they walked from the parking area to their apartment. And after a supper she forced down but didn't taste, she edged close to panic when he took out the trash and was gone longer than she expected.

"Some dog made a mess of the trash rack," he explained. "I cleaned it up."

She didn't want to watch television, or read, or do anything but be with him. She needed his nearness, needed to lock her arms around him and to have him hold her. Later, in bed, Sue burst into sobs and clutched him to her until she fell asleep.

They awoke to a bright dawn, still in each other's arms.

"Are you sure you're ready to go back to work?" he asked.

"Yes." Her jaw was set. Yesterday was behind them, and she wasn't going to let herself be trapped by her own fear. "Yes, I'm going to work."

Today was one of those obscure holidays—State Flag

Day or something—which city departments had off but private business did not. He dropped her off at Castleton. "You be a good girl now, and check everything out before you act on it."

"Where will you be?"

"I'm not sure. I'll stop for a second cup of coffee somewhere, I guess—collect myself. Then I'll be back in the apartment all afternoon."

Days like this always seemed strange, with her working and him roaming around feeling a little guilty for no reason.

"You be good," she said. Then she took his face in both hands and kissed him hard. "I love you, Don."

He almost tossed it away with a wisecrack, but realized just in time that this was one of those moments you don't joke about. He held her back by her hand as she moved to walk to the entrance. Their eyes met. There was nothing to say. Their eyes said it all.

He took the Ford slowly up Mill Street, then over to Country Boulevard, where he had put up the poster for Sid Harte. The poster was gone. A summer storm had probably ripped it from the pole. He turned north on Warren Road and let the car take him through the fields and strips of woods that hadn't yet fallen to the developers' bulldozers. Here and there, a scattering of new flat-faced tract houses spotted the gentle hills, but you could still pretend this would stay farming country.

Then he realized where he was going. It was as if he'd planned it, but he hadn't. He was on this road through some kind of Ouija Board logic: pressure here, counterpressure there, until the pointer spelled out the words you wanted . . . the place you wanted. He had put the Ford on the road to Clairmont. To his father.

Calvin Ellison wasn't as tall as Don remembered

him. It had been almost eight months! But he wasn't short, either; a tanned man of muscle and sinew with thin gray hair that fell over his forehead as he bent down for a rag on which to wipe his greasy hands. He had been up to his elbows in the tractor engine when Don drove into the farmyard. In his khaki work trousers and faded red shirt, he looked like a handyman.

"Your mother's over to town for groceries," Calvin Ellison said without a greeting. "She'll be sorry she missed you."

"I'm sorry to miss her, too. But I came to see you."

"Me?"

"I think so."

"Either you did or you didn't. I've no time for people who don't know their minds." Here came that all-too-familiar cold shell that seemed to come between them whenever they tried to talk together. Don determined to push on past it.

"There's no one else."

His father studied him curiously. "There's your wife."

"That's not the same. She's like me. We're up against something we barely understand. I thought maybe . . . maybe you could help."

Ellison laid the rag across the tractor's hood but kept his hard gray eyes on Don's face. "You seen fit to pull out of here and move into Millbury when I needed you to run this place with me. Would have been all yours one day if you'd taken an interest in it. Now I don't know what to do with it when I'm too old to work it. Sell to the developers, I suppose, and live out my years on the money. You've come back to ask me for help?

There's none to give. It's all been put in the land, in the barn, and the twenty head of Holstein. I haven't got a spare dollar—"

"Not money. I didn't come for money."

"What then?"

"To talk."

His father frowned at him. "To talk? What kind of advice might I have that would be of use to you? I thought you knew it all."

Don stuck his hands in his pockets and paced in front of his car, kicking a piece of gravel with the side of his shoe. "That was a dumb attitude," he said. "I've learned things since then."

"But not enough, I guess. Else you wouldn't be here." His father's tone was still rock hard.

"I'm beginning to realize that nobody ever learns enough."

Calvin Ellison leaned back against the long snout of his battered tractor. A crow cawed out in the pasture. "Looks like that's one thing we might agree on," he said slowly.

He reached into his shirt pocket with two gnarled fingers and pulled out a pack of little cigars. "You want one of these?"

This was the first time his father had ever offered him a smoke. "No, thanks," Don said.

"Just as well." Ellison lit up and cocked his head high to exhale a long blue stream into the light breeze. "What's on your mind?"

Of the several people he might have discussed this with, Don realized, he'd chosen the one man with whom he'd had trouble talking all his life. He could have tried Sue's father again, but he knew where

Walter Wallace stood, and he didn't like it. He could have gone to Charlie Pegler or Hobie Hasfeld, but now they were part of what was going on.

He took a long breath. There was something reassuring in the rich smell of damp earth, the sharp odor of the cow barn, the faint sweetness of his mother's carefully tended flower garden edging the clapboard house.

He knew his father hated long-winded explanations. "The city has told each of us to kick back part of our pay. If I do it, I keep my job. If I don't, I'll probably lose it. But what they are asking is wrong. Everybody knows that, but they go along with it because that's how it's always been."

His father raised a foot to the front wheel of the tractor. "You need the job?"

"I'll say I do."

"But you don't like the price. A lot of things come pretty cheap in this world. Maybe it's worth it to you to pay off to keep the job."

"Even when I know it's dead wrong to do that?"

Ellison leaned on his upraised knee. "Plenty of people figure everything's got a price on it. It's just a matter of whether you want to pay it or not. And everybody starts off with some kind of . . . well, principles. Some sell them cheap, some sell them high. A few don't ever sell them."

Don frowned. "I'm not sure—"

"Not sure I'm telling you anything? I can't. How can I tell you what to do? That's something you got to decide for yourself. You know that."

"Can't you just tell me what you think?"

Calvin Ellison flipped away his little cigar butt and stuffed his hands in his pockets. "I don't know anything about your job or what it really means to you. I guess I don't really know a whole lot about you, and I'm sorry for that. You're a hard worker. And you stay out of trouble. A lot of people never manage even that much."

Don's face froze. He'd made a mistake coming here. Too many grim years and too many failures had made his father as stern as his life had been. Don would never be able to get through the shell. He turned away.

"Wait . . . Don. Maybe it'd help if I told you there should be no price high enough to buy out a man. Once he's sold out, I doubt he ever gets back all his self-respect."

Don looked back at his father for a long moment. Then he said, "I think that's what I came to hear."

"That little girl you married, she all right?"

"She's fine, Dad." He moved toward the car. "You take care of yourself."

"Your mother'll be sorry she missed you."

"I'll tell Sue you said hello." He drove away quickly, but he took some of his father's stubborn strength with him. Not until now had he known what he had to do.

CHAPTER 9

THE UNOFFICIAL committee of revolt had gotten started long before Don realized there was such a group. It had begun the day Charlie Pegler had called them into his office one at a time to ask about Hobie Hasfeld's newspaper story. That tense morning, Pegler had talked to Al Hill, Kent Watters, Eddie Koslowski, and Don. Then there had followed Kent's guarded comments on the lawn behind the Department of Streets Building at lunch. "Eddie and I are with you," he'd said, as if Don had been looking for support.

Don had expected to be alone in his protest, but now he had allies he'd never asked for. He scrunched uncomfortably in a cheap easy chair in the small living room of Gil's apartment and listened to Gil outline his plans in excited, high-pitched bursts.

"Strength in numbers, see. That's what this is all about. That's why I asked all of you to come over here tonight." He yelled over his shoulder, "Hey, Lila! What's the holdup on the drinks, kid?"

Don glanced at Eddie Koslowski, sprawled in a corner chair with one leg hooked over a chair arm. Strange to see Eddie here. He was older by far than any of them. He'd combed his pale hair straight back and wore a neat little green bow tie with his yellow shirt.

"Look," Gil went on. "There's four of us. Four of us who won't go along with the kickback. If we hang in there, some others will go along with us. Maybe half the department. And The Man Downstairs can't fire half the department."

Kent Watters spoke up from the other end of the blue-and-white-striped sofa. "Half of the department, Gil? What makes you think we'd get anything like that kind of backing?" He twitched back his long hair with a jerk of his head and pulled at the collar of his lavender sports shirt. "I think you're a shade optimistic."

"A shade?" Eddie threw in. "More like a whole set of drapes!"

"Beers!" Gil brayed toward the kitchen. "C'mon, Lila!"

Kent nodded at Don. "What do you think? Can you picture half of the drafting room telling Charlie Pegler to stuff it?"

Time for honesty, Don decided. "I can't picture a single one of you telling him that."

A mutter of protest met his words. "What kind of a thing is that to say?" Eddie snorted. "We're all here, aren't we?"

"Let me say what I want to say. All three of you have at least a couple of years in. You've kicked back before. You know the system. Why should you decide now that you're going to buck it?"

"Sure, we know the score, and we've paid up in the past," Kent agreed. "But somewhere the line has to be drawn. And we've decided this is the time."

"And nobody's ever had the guts to report a word about the kickback system to the newspapers until you came along," Gil said.

"Look, Gil, I never said I had any part in that story."

"Two and Two. They don't add up to anyone but you. Am I right, or am I right?"

In the long pause that followed, Lila Greenwood swung around the entrance to the kitchen, a tray of foaming beer glasses in her hands. She was a slim girl with stringy black hair. You could find younger versions of her at any high-school dance, quiet to the point of being sullen. It was hard to determine whether she simply wasn't bright, didn't care about much of anything—or was smarter than any of them imagined and silently drank in everything around her that might be of personal use. Don favored the last analysis, and he never quite trusted tall, thin Lila Greenwood.

"To the decline and fall of The Man Downstairs," Gil announced, holding his glass high. "May he collapse like a bureaucratic balloon."

"I'll drink to that," Eddie agreed.

The brew was bitter cold, and Don took a few swallows, though he was no beer lover.

"Well?" Gil shot at him suddenly.

"Well what?"

"It *was* you who talked to that reporter, wasn't it?"

"You seem to know all about it, Gil."

"That settles it then. A toast to the only guy in the room with real initiative."

Kent frowned. "I think the fact that we're here at all shows initiative. Why don't you cut out the rah-rah,

Gil, and get on with what we came here for."

"Okay, okay, Kent. Well, I see it this way. Friday is the day we're supposed to turn in our contributions, right? So through this week, we talk to as many of the clowns in the drafting room as we think will go along with us. Get them to sit tight. And we sit tight ourselves, really tight. None of us gives a dime."

"I don't know," Eddie said. "That's asking for a whole lot of guts from a whole lot of people. Some of those guys are getting close to retirement—like Al Hill. They aren't going to do anything that would mess them up."

"So don't talk with those particular guys," Gil said. "Just hit the good probables. We know who they are. We get them to hold out, and we've got it made. Right, Don?"

Don turned his glass in his fingers. There was something about this that made him uneasy. The plan was simple, as a good plan should be. And Gil was right in pointing out that if enough drafting-room personnel simply refused to pay, The Man Downstairs would be in a tough spot. If he actually did fire half of his design force, the scandal probably would spill over city boundaries to the state capital. Yet there was something wrong with all this, some angle . . . .

It was Gil. The excitable redhead was trying to ride to glory on somebody else's horse. Hadn't Gil told him to shut up and pay when Don had first muttered how he felt about the kickback? Now that Don appeared to have some sort of ball rolling, Gil was grabbing for fame of his own.

"So all three of you are with me," Don said. "Well, I thank you for that. It's a help." And it was. Just the fact that some others were willing to take a chance and fight

69

the system was reassuring. He doubted that half of the drafting room—that even a quarter of the drafting room—would follow their lead. But at least there would be four of them.

Gil spoke up quickly. "Great, Don. Glad you go along with the plan."

"I didn't say that, Gil. I don't think you're going to get anywhere at all talking with anybody else in that drafting room. If there were more of us, we would already have heard from them."

"How would they know whom to talk to?"

"How did Eddie and Kent know? It's just us four, and that's it."

"I don't believe that," Gil argued, "and starting tomorrow, I'll prove it."

The Man Downstairs paced his office in jumpy strides. What in the devil was going on up there in the drafting room? At ten forty-five, Billy Crimm had called from his desk outside Charlie Pegler's office.

"Some kind of buzz up here."

"Buzz? What's that mean?" Blast Crimm's cut-up sentences.

"Dunno. Something's going on. Some guys going table to table with a message of some kind, I think."

"Who?"

Crimm's voice dropped to a muffled mumble. He was holding his hand over his mouth and the mouthpiece. "Watters, Koslowski, and Barber."

"Tell Pegler to tell Corrigan to tell them to get back to work."

"Can't do that," Crimm pointed out. "Can't give Pegler an order from you."

Crimm was right, of course. If Munroe used Crimm

as a messenger boy, Pegler might tumble to Crimm's real assignment in the drafting room. And as far as Munroe knew, nobody was aware of Crimm's actual purpose there.

"Keep tabs on what's going on. We'll meet for lunch."

"Better not leave together."

"That's exactly right, Billy. You be at Henley's Seafood House at twelve fifteen. I'll find you."

Munroe stopped pacing and looked at his watch. Noon. Finally. He slapped his crumpled madras hat on his bald head, told his secretary he'd be back in an hour, and hurried to his car. He pulled into Henley's parking lot just twelve minutes later. Inside, Billy Crimm already sat in a poorly lighted booth in a far corner.

They ordered quickly. "Got to be back there by one," Crimm warned, "or there may be questions."

"You'll get back." Munroe ran his fingers along his cheeks and rubbed his long jaw. "So what have you been able to find out?"

Big Billy Crimm tossed The Man Downstairs a quick grin. "Found out what's going on. Like you asked. Picked up a little here, a little there, until I had it all."

"And?"

"Ellison again. Got the other three running a campaign for him. Idea is to get as many as he can to refuse to contribute Friday."

"The other three are Watters, Koslowski, and Barber?"

"That's right."

"Good work, Billy. Now let's enjoy our lunch."

Forty-five minutes later, Munroe strode back into his

office and shut the door behind him. He used the outside line that didn't go through the office switchboard.

"Chief Stone's office," a secretary answered.

"Munroe, Department of Streets." This was the weak link in their phone conversations, but Glen had assured him that the secretary neither logged incoming calls nor had any imagination whatever.

Glen Stone came on the line, clearing his throat noisily. "Carleton? What can I do for you today?"

"It's our friend with the dirty license plate, Glen. I don't think he's been convinced."

"I see. I'll pass the word, Carleton."

"Do that, Glen. How's Mary?"

"She's fine. I'll tell her that you asked."

Munroe hung up, reached for a cigar, and sat back in his leather swivel chair to light up. Just when things were going smoothly, it always seemed that somebody like Ellison came along to screw them up. But there were ways to handle such problems, and he'd never yet run up against a troublemaker who couldn't be bought off or scared into line.

Ellison was a special case, though, because of his connection with Walt Wallace. It wouldn't do to push him around directly, but you'd think the kid would take a hint or two. The license-plate ploy had been safe enough, but the boy apparently had been too dumb or too stubborn to realize what was going on. By Friday, though, what Ellison was going to go through would convince even a moron that he couldn't buck the whole city.

The police officer was young. He wore long sideburns and a sour look. The bill of his cap almost

72

touched the bridge of his nose, and he tilted his head back to squint down at Don.

"You were doing thirty-seven in a thirty-five zone, buster."

"My speedometer said under thirty-five."

"You want to argue it out in court against my radar? License and registration, Ellison."

This one already knew his name, too.

"Ticket's going to cost you twenty-five plus two bucks for each mile over the limit. Twenty-nine in all. Either send in the check or show up at traffic court two weeks from Tuesday."

As the officer returned to his cruiser and moved down Mill Street, Don pulled a small notebook from his pocket. "July 27," he wrote. "Mill Street at Second Ave. Ticket for 37 in 35 zone. Officer J. Mangrum."

That was his second entry. The first he had penciled in last night "July—" he'd forgotten the exact date. "Ash Street. Dirty license place." Unfortunately, he hadn't at that time decided to make it a point to read the name on the little chrome plate over the officer's right pocket.

Tuesday, he walked out of the Watkins Pharmacy, where he had stopped to get a bottle of shampoo for Sue. A ticket fluttered beneath his windshield wiper. Parking violation: more than six inches from the curb. He checked. They had him by maybe half an inch. The car in front of his was more than a foot from the stone curb line. "July 28," he wrote in the notebook. "Parking ticket. 6½ inches from curb."

By Thursday night, there were two more entries in the little blue plastic notebook. "July 29, speeding up to run yellow light." He had run the light, but he hadn't increased his speed at all. "Officer J. Wirts."

And: "July 30, car emitting excessive exhaust. Officer L. Littleton."

"They're out to drown me in ticket tape," he told Sue. "I know it, and they know that I know it. If they keep at it, I'll spend the rest of my life in traffic court and repair shops."

Friday morning, just after he dropped Sue off at Castleton, a police cruiser glided alongside at a light.

"Hey, Ellison! One of your brake-light lenses looks like it's cracked, but we'll let you go today. Just today. It's a special day—you know what I mean?"

Don knew. Today was contribution day. Today the money was due, and today he would learn whether or not Gil knew what he was talking about. But Don flipped out his notebook and made the sixth entry. He'd recognized the officer. J. Mangrum again.

The drafting room, usually noisy with chair scrapings, pencil grindings, and general jabber as it opened for business, was oddly quiet as he and Gil folded their drafting-table covers. "You can feel it," Gil said. "Something's going to happen today. That's for sure."

It happened fifteen minutes later. Charlie Pegler answered the phone in his glass cage, nodded, and walked across the entire drafting room to Kent Watters' table. Kent looked up as Charlie spoke, turned pale, then slid off his drafting stool and headed downstairs.

Ten minutes later he returned grim-faced and motioned to Eddie Koslowski. Eddie laid down his drafting pencil and triangle, compressed his lips, and went downstairs. He was back in twelve minutes, as subdued as Kent had been, and he came straight for Gil.

"Man Downstairs wants to see you."

Gil licked dry lips. "What's going on, Eddie? You look like you've been dragged through a soda straw."

The older draftsman's face flushed red. "Just go see him, Gil."

The mouthy redhead shrugged at Don, stuck his hands in his pockets, and sauntered to the stairs. Leave it to Gil, Don thought. Always that little show of false strength.

Like the others, Gil was back in a few minutes. His bravado had left him. "Now he wants to see you," he said in a flat voice.

"What's happening down there?"

Gil's eyes slid away. "You'll find out. Go on, get it over with."

CHAPTER 10

Don stood up, shoved his drafting stool aside, and walked to the stairs. Everything had gone wrong. He could feel it. His knees were suddenly rubbery. It's only a talk with a city bureaucrat, he told himself angrily. Pull yourself back into one piece. But the bureaucrat was The Man Downstairs, and the creeping fear wouldn't go away.

At the bottom of the steps he turned and walked down the long hallway toward the rear of the building, past the offices where desk calculators whirred and snapped out construction-cost estimates; where payroll clerks computed paycheck deductions, seniority increments, and leave times; where a group of people fell silent as he passed them at a coffee station.

Then he was at the door. The middle-aged secretary raised her thin eyebrows. "Ellison? Go on in. Mr. Munroe expects you."

That was a laugh. Munroe sent for him like a general

ordering a soldier to report. Don walked through the secretary's little area and into the corner office.

It was larger than he had expected, with windows on two sides. The bright July morning sun streamed across a beige rug, splashed the dark-stained furniture with gold. There was a scattering of hard-backed walnut chairs, a low bookcase along one paneled wall. The two windowless walls were decorated with dozens of framed mementos of Munroe's political past: a photo of him with Senator McGovern when the Senator had campaigned in Millbury; an equally large photo of Munroe shaking hands with vice-presidential candidate Spiro Agnew; photos of Munroe with three of the state's past governors and two former Millbury mayors; citations from the Rotary, Kiwanis, and Lions clubs; certificates of appreciation from a whole range of city- and state-level department heads. The wall display was designed to show power and influence, and it added to Don's uneasiness.

"Sit down, Ellison."

The order came from behind the big glass-topped walnut desk that angled across the far corner of the room, its surface clear except for a pen set, a polished wooden box, and a large manila envelope. The desk was flanked on one side by the city flag and by the state flag on the other. It gave Don the quick impression that he had somehow stumbled into the office of the President of the United States just as the TV cameras were about to go on.

That feeling was quickly erased as he looked at the man in the chair behind the desk. He had a long horselike head, bald but for a gray fringe. The face tapered to a heavy chin. The eyes, set too wide for that oblong face, were like blue glass chips, unblinking. Cold.

"I told you to sit down, Ellison."

Don couldn't take his eyes off that face as he walked across the office and took the chair across the desk from The Man Downstairs.

Munroe held a large file card between his fingertips. He studied it for endless moments. Then he looked straight into Don's stare.

"Do you like your job, Ellison?"

The constant use of his last name began to hit Don like a slap. He hesitated. He could throw away everything he'd worked for by the way he answered the loaded question. "I'm . . . I'm in no position to say that I don't."

Don could see that wasn't what Munroe expected to hear. The Man Downstairs scowled. "You understand what's expected of you up in the drafting room?"

"To do the work that's assigned to me."

"That's right, and I understand that you do that well. There's a future for you here, Ellison, providing you do the *total* job, not just the minimum job. You understand what I'm telling you?"

"Not quite." Don's voice was strong, but his palms were clammy on the chair arms. Where was all that courage he'd thought he had brought downstairs with him?

"This is a city agency, a political animal as well as a service department. I didn't set it up that way, and I make no judgments about it. My job is to see that this department functions the way the city wants it to function. That's all. Now we've been operating smoothly for years, and we intend to continue to operate that way for years to come. But every now and then, some dreamy-eyed reformer gets on the payroll and causes a certain amount of irritation."

Munroe let his words hang heavy as he chose a cigar from the polished humidor on his desk, clipped off its end with a small scissors from a desk drawer, and lit it with no hurry. He's letting me stew, Don realized. Nothing this guy does is casual. Everything is planned for effect.

"I know your type, Ellison. I've dealt with it before, and I even admire it. You're young, honest as the day is long, something of an idealist. Then you begin to discover that the world is run by practical men, not idealists. It comes as something of a shock. So you decide to revolt. That's understandable. I felt the same way when I was your age."

Shades of Charlie Pegler. He's setting me up, Don thought.

Munroe's voice hardened. "Then I grew up. I realized that's the way things are, and that's the way things work best. I wasn't going to be able to change it, so I got with it. And I think I've come a long, long way with that philosophy. I think you'll go a long way if you get with it, too. You understand what I'm saying?"

"I understand what you're saying." That was the same non-answer he'd given to Charlie Pegler weeks ago. Charlie had delivered the same lecture. The difference was that way down underneath, Charlie didn't like the system. But Munroe *was* the system. And so they both carried the same message: the world is run by politics, and politics isn't always a nice, clean business, so relax and enjoy it while you can.

"Fine. I thought we would see eye to eye once we sat down and talked it out." Munroe took a long drag on his cigar, stuck out his lower lip, and blew the smoke upward. He reached into the manila envelope and pulled out three packets of money bound with rubber bands.

"Watters," he said as he tossed one back on the desk. "Koslowki." He tossed the second. "Barber." The third pack of bills dropped across the first two.

Don was stunned. It was as if honesty and word of honor lay there dead among the three piles of money.

"Now you see how things are, Ellison. You're all alone in this mess you've stirred up. Your three friends who promised to support you obviously never intended to do any such thing once the chips were down. You've been taken. You're out on a limb all by yourself. If you want to take credit for a nice try, I'll give you credit: nice try." Munroe's bent smile mocked him. Then the long face tightened. "Now let me have your contribution."

This was the moment Don had dreaded for so long. This was the time when the decision really counted, not back when he knew there were a lot of weeks to go and when talk against the system had been cheap. What would truly affect his—and Sue's life was what he would do right now, right here in Munroe's office. It had all worked down to what he would say in the next few seconds.

He stared at the money on the desk. Some support he'd gotten from those three! He'd made his stand, and nobody, not one of those guys up there, had stood with him when the real decision came. He had every reason to come down off his soapbox now, kick in his money, and save himself. In a year or so he'd be out of here anyway, working on a far better job away from Millbury.

"Well, Ellison?" The cigar had risen to an upward victory tilt. "Are you with us?"

With us? With anonymous phone calls? With using the police department as a private pressure squad? With frightening employees into handing over their hard-earned money for political use?

"No, Mr. Munroe, I'm not with you. I didn't bring the money. I don't have it because I'm not going to contribute. It's wrong. You know it is. I know it is. And just because it's been done for years doesn't make it right."

He had said it. He had said it all. And his voice had stayed steady. Those weren't just words. He believed what he'd said, and he was sure he was right.

The cigar dropped below nose level. And it went out. Munroe's face was unreadable. "I expected more of you than that, Ellison. Big things." His voice was brittle, but he forced a cold smile. "Tell you what I can do for you. You take the weekend to think it over. Then, on Monday, you come in here with your contribution, and we'll strike this whole conversation from the record. Fair enough?"

"It won't make any difference," Don said. But he was confused. He'd expected some kind of lightning to strike him in his chair. Instead, The Man Downstairs seemed to be throwing him a last-minute life preserver. Or straw. Why would he do that?

"You're too smart a fellow not to know exactly what the score is, Ellison." Munroe's tone was confidential. The Man Downstairs stood up. "All right, get back to work. And make damned sure that you get back here Monday with your voluntary contribution."

Don returned to the drafting room fuming with anger

and frustration. He strode to his stool without returning Gil's look and tried to concentrate on the cross-section sheets.

"Some deal," Gil muttered beside him. "They really put the screws to a guy when the time comes, don't they?"

Don whirled toward him, his eyes blazing. "Or a guy says, 'Big bills or little ones?' when The Man Downstairs says 'pay up'! "

"Now hold on! There just wasn't anything else we could do."

"Come on, Gil. You never intended to do anything else. You and Kent and Eddie all brought your kickback money with you today. Three pockets full of cash. Why?"

Gil fixed his eyes on the point of his drafting pencil. "We . . . thought we could hold out, but just in case we couldn't—"

"You three were great, just great! You played it both ways all along the line. And you're the worst, Gil. You couldn't stand not being top dog when it looked like I might be getting somewhere. But when the crunch came, you turned out to be all mouth and no guts."

Gil said nothing. They worked in silence through the rest of the day while, one by one, every employee in the big drafting room slipped meekly downstairs to turn in his kickback.

The revolt was crushed. The drafting-room staff, like everyone else on the city's payroll, had no taste for fighting pressure from supervisors all the way up to who-knew-where, maybe even the Governor himself. They were trained to go along, and along they went.

Except for one.

CHAPTER 11

SATURDAY MORNING The Man Downstairs awoke at dawn. He hadn't slept well. There was something about that business yesterday with young Ellison that still bothered him. The way the kid had handled himself, maybe. He hadn't been arrogant, but at the same time he hadn't backed down an inch. People like that unsettled Munroe. He hadn't met many whom he couldn't eventually break. But Ellison had proved to be tougher than most.

Munroe pulled on his bathrobe and turned on the burner beneath the teakettle in the kitchen. When the water boiled, he made a cup of double-strong instant coffee and sipped it as he stood at the kitchen window and stared into the rain. He wasn't married. He'd never had time for it in his upward scramble from his parents' factory-worker row house to his stone residence here on Hunter's Hill.

He glanced up at the kitchen clock. Two hours until his housekeeper, Mrs. Mangrum, arrived. She was devoted to him, because he'd gotten her son a job with the police department. He would shave and dress slowly. That would give him time to think out the problem with Ellison.

He left the empty cup in the sink, stuck his hands in his bathrobe pockets, and prowled the house in frustration. What did you do with a guy like Ellison? The anonymous phone calls hadn't seemed to affect him. Neither had the tightening of the screws by the police department.

What made the thing even more hairy was that Munroe wasn't totally sure of his ground. Suppose the kid's father-in-law did decide to run for a high city office and actually managed to win? Munroe would be in a fine spot if in the meantime he'd fired the kid without a cause that would stand up under investigation. Walt Wallace, as a city councilman, or—God forbid—as mayor, would nail Munroe's hide to a road sign.

So The Man Downstairs was in a bind. If Ellison held out and didn't get fired for it, that could be the beginning of the end—the crack in the wall that would bring the whole thing down on Munroe's head. Next time around there would be more employees refusing to pony up, then still more, until his department was out of control. The party would quickly decide that they could do without him.

He plunked into a chair facing the living room's picture window and watched the rain. Wasn't he making a giant out of one wet-behind-the-ears dumb kid who really didn't have much going for him when you stopped and thought about it? So Walt Wallace was making noises about running for office. So what? Walt hadn't made any move to run this time around, and a lot could happen between now and the next election, two years away.

The corner of Munroe's mouth twisted upward. When you got right down to it, Ellison was no more than an annoying buzz. A fly. And to get rid of a fly, all you needed was a swatter.

At nine fifteen, as Mrs. Mangrum began to wax the black-and-white kitchen linoleum, Munroe dialed the phone in his study. He was dressed now, and the doubts of the early morning had resolved themselves into action. He hated doubt, and he liked action.

"Glen? Sorry to call you at home. Look, I appreciate what you've been doing about our mutual problem. But I don't think it has been as effective as we'd hoped. You follow me?"

Police Chief Glen Stone cleared his throat. "We've got to take care, Carleton. Everything's got to be in the line of duty, follow correct procedures." His heavy voice lowered to nearly a raspy whisper. "I don't want to find myself in a courtroom because some idiot patrolman has gone overboard. It could happen, Carleton."

"Don't you have control over your own people?"

"More than you, it would seem. Aren't you asking me for help with one of yours?"

Munroe's mouth tightened. He'd left himself wide open for that one. "Don't get funny, Glen. This thing needs one good push—nothing that can get us in hot water, you understand, just one good scare into that boy. He'll get the point like any other intelligent citizen. You got the picture?"

"Like I say, Carleton, it's hard to tell how far the boys might—"

"It's not hard, Glen. Just tell them." And Munroe

hung up, feeling some satisfaction for the first time today.

The Ford rolled smoothly through the downpour as Don turned off Country Boulevard onto Mill Street. It was past midnight, and the street was empty. The overhead lights cast yellow shimmers on the glistening blacktop, but their illumination was blotted up by the dark storefronts.

"Hobie didn't think you had much of a story, did he?" Sue said, staring into the night beyond the windshield wipers.

"He's right. He pointed out that I refused to contribute and all that happened to me was that I got an extension of the deadline until Monday. That's not exactly exciting newspaper copy. I guess we'll have to wait to see what happens Monday."

"What do you think will?" Her voice was small, as if she were afraid to hear his answer.

"I'll go in there and tell The Man Downstairs that I'm sticking to my guns, and in a few weeks or months I'll get a letter that outlines the last-in, first-out policy. It'll say that since the department's budget is tight, I'm out."

"But you can protest."

"Who to? And about what?" Yesterday Don had been full of fight, but now he was no longer so sure of himself. Not after tonight's conversation at Hobie Hasfeld's apartment. Hobie had wanted fireworks to write about, not smoldering punk. The fact that Don had been stopped six times by the police certainly looked like out-and-out harassment, but it could have been coincidence.

86

Don had snorted at that.

No, it could have been, Hobie insisted, and for his story to be effective, he had to have that final clincher. Where was it? As far as Hobie could see, the clincher at the moment was that when Don had refused to pay up, he'd gotten an extension to Monday. What had begun as front-page crusade, Hobie said, had turned into a page-four story about one disgruntled city employee.

"Is that how I look to you?" Don had challenged.

"No, but that's how you'll look to our readers, no matter how I write it. The whole thing has become too subtle now, too much an in-thing between you and Munroe. It would have helped if those other three guys had stuck by you."

"It sure would have. I found out a whole lot about human nature."

"Yeah," Hobie said. "Guts don't transfer easily."

"So what do we need to make a story?"

"The smoking gun!"

"The what?"

"Something illegal that can definitely be tied in with your refusal to go along with the macing policy."

"Oh, wonderful," Don said. "You're saying that we can't do a thing unless the roof falls in on us."

"I'm afraid that's about it, ol' buddy. Not much of a story the way it stands, but I'm always ready to hear from you."

Don scowled. "I thought you were supposed to be an investigative reporter."

"Every reporter should be an investigator, but my best lead can't give me anything solid to work on."

"Sorry. It's still an important story to me, but I can understand why it isn't front-page news anymore."

Hobie had nodded. "That's the way some things work out. But if there are any new developments—anything at all—call me. Anytime."

Now, driving back to their apartment from Hobie's, Don and Sue both felt a total letdown. The Department of Streets' kickback project had been successfully completed, with just one exception. When the moment of truth finally came, everyone had knuckled under and forked over the money. Everyone except Don, the lone and lonely holdout.

An odd thing had happened. After all the others had kicked in and become part of the system, Don was no longer in the club. He could feel that in the way Gil, Kent, and Eddie treated him at lunch on the lawn. Don was seeing a lot of backs out there behind the department building. He no longer belonged. The others' contributions had lined them up with the ins, and they avoided him without even realizing it. He was an outsider now, maybe even a threat.

Don was so caught up in his thoughts that the flashing lights had pulled close behind before he noticed them. Then the siren's scream bounced off Mill Street's black building fronts.

The blue-and-white swung around and knifed in to cut them off. Don stood on the brakes. The car squealed sidewise and shuddered to a stop, inches from the police cruiser's white fender.

The officers were at both doors, guns out, standing stiff and ready and dangerous.

"Out! Hands on your heads!"

"Wait a min—"

"Shut up! No talk. Face the car. Spread your legs. Hands on the roof."

He felt the officer's hands run down his body, down

his legs. Across the wet car roof, he could see the other policeman searching Sue.

"You're making one hell of a mistake," Don managed to say before the officer jolted his palm into Don's shoulder.

"Shut up. Reach for your wallet with two fingers. Slowly. Show me some I.D."

Don took out his driver's license and thrust it behind him. He wasn't scared now. As he had scrambled out of the car, he had seen something that changed his fright to boiling anger.

"Ellison, eh. All right, back in your vehicle and on your way."

No apology. No explanation. The police cruiser pulled away and disappeared down Mill Street.

Sue's voice was that of a terrified child. "What did they—" She choked back tears. "What did they do that for, Don?"

He was so angry that he had to struggle to keep his voice steady. "That was part of it, Sue, part of the plan to shut me up and push me back in line. The city departments are all one big coordinated fraternity."

"I didn't really believe—"

"Didn't believe the dirty license plate, the parking ticket, the speeding charges, the threat about the brake light? You believe it now?"

"I don't know what else they'd do all that for."

"Now you've got it!" His words came out like shots. He started the engine with a savage twist of the key, tramped on the accelerator, and threw the car into a screeching U-turn. Sue gasped and grabbed for the door handle.

"I'm tired of being shoved around, tired of being pushed into supporting a system I hate. I'm just plain tired of being scared. We're going back to Hobie's."

"To Hobie's?"

"That's right." His mouth was a tight line. "I'm going to tell him he can print anything he wants to."

The story broke Monday morning:

CITY EMPLOYEE BLOWS WHISTLE ON KICKBACK OPERATION

Donald R. Ellison, a resident of the Timberlane Apartments in North Millbury, revealed yesterday that he was the anonymous source of information this paper previously published concerning the city's alleged macing of Department of Streets personnel.

Ellison, 20, has been employed as a draftsman for the department since December. He stated in an interview that he and all other employees of the Department of Streets have been told to "kick back" stated percentages of their salaries to help finance candidates in the coming general election.

"I was told to come up with $260," he said. Asked if there were any threats accompanying the request, he said, "It's pretty well understood that you either pay up or get out."

Mr. Ellison said that he decided to speak out after being stopped by a Millbury police patrol car shortly after midnight Saturday. He and his wife, the former Susan Wallace, daughter of a prominent local attorney, were searched, then released without explanation.

90

Mr. Ellison said that the incident was the climax of a series of harassments by the Millbury Police Department, stemming from his refusal to make the political contribution.

"It's all tied in," he stated. "I think the idea is to scare me into line. It hasn't worked. I'm not scared. I'm mad."

A check with the Millbury police confirmed that Mr. Ellison and his wife had been detained on Mill Street at 12:09 A.M. Sunday. A department spokesman said the Ellisons were released when it was determined they were not the couple the police were searching for in connection with an automobile theft in nearby Clairmont.

Told of the police explanation, Mr. Ellison said, "I can't accept that. One of the officers was a J. Mangrum. I saw his nameplate. He had already stopped me twice before. It's impossible that he didn't recognize my car."

Officer Mangrum was not immediately available for comment.

The Man Downstairs sat behind his desk, his elbows on the chair arms, his fingers forming a tent beneath his chin. The phone jangled. He flinched at the sudden sound.

"Carleton, it's Glen."

"I've been expecting you, Glen."

"I thought maybe you'd call me."

"It wasn't *my* people who made that damned kid go to the newspaper, Glen. What in God's name were you trying to do?"

The chief's voice took on an edge. "Trying to do what you asked us to. I warned you how dangerous it could get. And that's just what's happened."

"What happened was that you couldn't control your men."

"It wasn't any of my men who blabbed to the paper, Carleton. Keep that in mind."

Stone had a point there.

"Dump that kid, Carleton. The only reason the paper is listening to him is because he's a Department of Streets employee. Take that away from him, and he's just another griper who got fired."

Munroe twisted his face into a sour grimace. "I wish it was that easy. If I fire him now that the story has been in the paper, how am I going to look to the press? That would just confirm what he's been saying."

"But if you keep him on, how many more hotshots in your department will decide they can get away with the same thing? You can have a revolt on your hands the next time you ask for contributions. Take my advice. Find some sort of excuse and drop that kid."

"It's a problem."

"Face it, Carleton. For both our sakes." The connection was broken.

Face it, sure. He would, of course, but first he had to think this thing out carefully. As he'd told the police chief, he had a problem.

CHAPTER 12

"YOU WOULDN'T take my advice, would you!" Walter Wallace stopped pacing around the apartment's small living room and flung his hands in the air. "Now you've dragged me into this mess!"

Don stared up at him. "I've gotten you into it?"

"Carleton Munroe called me this afternoon and told me you were a noncooperative employee with a negative attitude. He asked me to talk to you, to pound some sense into your head. To save your job. Otherwise, he's going to have to fire you. How do you think that's going to look? My own son-in-law fired by the city!"

"What do you think I should do?" Don asked. He knew what he was going to do, but he wanted to hear Wallace's answer.

"I think you should apologize to Munroe, make the contribution, and get yourself back into line."

"Isn't this whole thing coming out backwards?" Don asked. "I've been told to hand over kickback money.

I've been hassled by the police. Saturday night Sue and I were treated like two criminals. Now my own father-in-law has been pressured to pressure me. And you say I'm the one who should apologize!"

"Don, it's just good politics."

"For me or for you?" Don shot back.

Wallace appealed to Sue and her mother on the sofa. "Obviously I can't make any headway. One of you talk to him."

Sue's eyes blazed. "You weren't stopped by those police officers, Daddy. You weren't searched like I was. Don's right. It's all part of a plan to make him pay the money."

"That's all it takes, Sue. All this ridiculous trouble would be over with if he'd just do that."

"I don't want him to, Daddy. I'm ready to fight right along with him."

Wallace rubbed his hand across his forehead. "I can't believe I'm hearing this from my own daughter. For Pete's sake, Elizabeth, talk some sense into her!"

Elizabeth Wallace kept her eyes on the handkerchief twisted in her fingers. "Walter, I'm not sure I agree with you either."

Wallace's voice rose a notch higher. "I can't believe this! Doesn't at least one of you see the thing from the practical side?"

He sat down abruptly on the arm of the sofa and began to tick off the points of his argument on his thin fingers. "One, Don's trying to buck a system that's been operating this way for decades. Two, nobody else went along with him. Three, his stand can very well mess up any political career I might want to try. Four—"

"Don," Elizabeth Wallace interrupted, "is it the

money? Because, if you don't have it, we can easily lend or even give it to you."

"It's no longer only the money. It's the whole principle of the thing. Why can't everyone see that?"

His mother-in-law tried a weak smile. "I think I understand. I just wanted to make sure."

"Don't worry, Mother," Sue put in. "We're sure."

"Well, you'll go straight down the drain being sure of yourselves," Wallace snorted. "You'll be an oddball all your life, Don, if you don't learn how to bend a little when you should."

"I don't believe that," Don said. "I don't believe you can't change things that are wrong. Somebody has to try."

"All right, I'll agree that you're an honest kid. I'll give you that. But you're too darned naive. Too bad you never went to college. All that determination of yours could have been channeled into so many useful directions."

"And I'd probably be clever enough to stay out of the city's hair," Don snapped. "Is that what you're saying?"

Elizabeth Wallace touched his knee. "Don, that isn't fair!"

"None of this is fair! That's the whole point. But only Sue can see it."

Wallace shook his head slowly. "You think anybody in this country—I mean really important people—got where they are by being Eagle Scouts all the way up the ladder? Life isn't like that anymore. Do you want to be somebody or not? It can't be done the way you're going about it."

"I never said I wanted to be a senator or even a city councilman," Don flared. "I just want to be a street designer. I didn't ask to be in the middle of this stupid fight. I just didn't want to pay crooked money."

Wallace looked at Don for a long silent moment. His wife cleared her throat nervously. Finally he said, "I wish it were that simple. I could have helped you to be a name in this town, Don. But you're throwing it all away." He shrugged. "I don't know what kind of job I can get you next. It's not going to be so easy."

Don struggled to hold his temper. "I don't need your help. I can find my own—"

The telephone in the kitchen broke into the discussion.

"I'll get it," Don said, glad for an excuse to get out of the room.

"He's totally impossible," Wallace fumed. "Can't you do anything with him, Sue?"

"You just don't understand, Daddy. You should be proud of him."

"Proud! He's not only blowing his own future. He's messing up mine!"

"Walter," Elizabeth Wallace said, "don't you think you've said enough about the way Sue and Don are trying to live their lives? I think it's time to go home."

Wallace stared at her. "All right, that does it. I've said all I can say. Whatever happens from now on—"

Don's expression in the kitchen doorway stopped him. "That was Hobie on the phone," Don said. His voice was odd.

"Who?"

"The reporter we know, Daddy," Sue said. "Don, what's happened?"

"Hobie said it just came over the press wire from the state capital. The Governor is appointing a committee to investigate the macing charges here in Millbury. They're going to begin hearings in two weeks."

Walter Wallace's face sagged. "My God, Don, what have you done to this town?"

Don faced them with a determination they hadn't seen in him before. "Mr. Wallace . . . Walter . . . I hope I've done it some good!"

CHAPTER 13

THE MAN DOWNSTAIRS picked up the phone in his study, settled back into his reclining chair—a Christmas gift from department employees—reached for his coffee cup, and said, "Hello?" He was expecting a call from Billy Crimm. Billy was angling for a raise, and Munroe was prepared to give him part of what he wanted but not the whole thirty cents an hour he was asking for.

The five words from the other end of the line jerked Munroe upright. His left hand banged against the cup, and coffee sloshed across the magazine table.

The smooth voice said, "This is the Governor speaking."

The Governor! He would have been better prepared to hear from the Mayor; in fact, he wondered why he hadn't. But the Governor! In person—not through an assistant or by letter, but by surprise on the phone like this.

"Nice to hear from you, Governor," he said in a fluster, trying hard to pull himself together.

"I understand you have a problem down there. As a matter of fact, we both have a problem. You have backed me into quite a corner."

"I certainly didn't mean to, Governor. I tried every way I could to head it off."

"So I noticed, Munroe," the Governor said dryly. "After that statewide news coverage, there was very little I could do but order an investigation. State funds help support city departments in Millbury, so I had no choice."

Munroe was silent. He remembered the Governor during the first campaign, a quiet professor of history, an unassuming man ready to take orders from the professionals running his campaign. But that had changed the day he was inaugurated. He had turned into a leader, ready to give orders to the same men who had told him how to win. One of them had been Munroe.

"I'm appointing a committee of three. Two state legislators and a representative of the City of Millbury. I thought you might have a recommendation."

A smile twitched at the corners of Munroe's thin mouth. So the Governor did remember some of his political debts after all. This investigation might not shape up too badly. The Governor was actually giving him a chance to get his own man on the investigating committee. He had let himself hope that perhaps the Governor's well-publicized committee hearings were going to be just public eyewash. That idea had been nibbling at him most of the week, but he had pushed it away because it was too much even to wish for. Yet here was the Governor himself on the phone, handing Munroe one of the committee appointments.

"I could suggest a good man for you to consider, Governor. Fine legal mind. He's a lawyer, as a matter of fact, and a city councilman."

"A member of the party?"

"Of course, Governor,"

"And up for reelection, I presume."

"He happens to be, yes."

"I didn't think you'd miss a chance for publicity for one of your people, Munroe."

"Now, I didn't say he was one of my people, Governor." Munroe allowed the Governor to hear a wry chuckle. This was more like the old days.

"Let me put it this way, then. Is he *known* to be one of your people?"

"He's one of the most popular men on the Millbury City Council. He pulled a seventy-three percent vote the last time around, and he hasn't made any mistakes in office."

"Sounds like a possibility. Who is he?"

"Sid Harte."

"Oh, the fellow who managed to get the state to help finance the Mill Street Shopping Mall. Very persuasive. Yes, I think he'll help balance my committee."

Munroe decided to take a chance. "May I ask who else will be on it?" He held his breath.

The Governor hesitated. Then he said, "It won't be officially announced until tomorrow, but I know I can trust your discretion."

"Of course, Governor."

"I've asked State Senator Sylvestro to serve, and I've appointed State Senator Alexander as chairman."

"Jimmy Alexander from Centerham?"

"You know him?"

"His automobile agency was one of the bidders on the city's contract for new police cars last fall."

Munroe heard a sharp intake of breath at the other end. "Was he the winning bidder?" the Governor asked.

"No."

"Thank heaven for that. You had me worried for a minute, Munroe. This investigation has to look good."

Those were the key words Munroe had been hoping to hear. *Look good.* The Governor was concerned with appearances, maybe more with appearances than with results, Munroe thought. And he was going to accept Sid Harte as the third man on the investigating committee. Things might not be so black after all.

"I'm with you all the way, Governor," Munroe said. "I'm just sorry that this thing got out of hand. The newspapers have blown the whole situation way out of proportion, as usual. I'm sure you're aware of that. It's just one young kid who—"

"Whatever the cause," the Governor cut in, "it's extremely inconvenient."

"Yes, sir."

"Let's hope it's no more than that."

"Don't worry, Governor."

"Be careful, Munroe."

He hung up with his stomach beginning to knot. He'd thought he had it made when the Governor had agreed to accept Sid Harte, but then came the warning. How did you read a conversation like that?

He went to the kitchen for a sponge, mopped up the spilled coffee, then sank back into his chair with a frown. He couldn't relax now. He reached for the phone and dialed.

"Sid? Carleton Munroe." They went through the usual exchange of pleasantries. "Sid, this is in confidence. The Governor is going to appoint you to the investigating committee for the Ellison thing. He'll probably be in touch with you tonight or early tomorrow."

"Me? Why me?" Harte's voice was a series of quacks.

"Because I suggested you." It never hurt to remind politicians where some of their clout came from.

"And the Governor accepted?"

"Yes, he did."

"Interesting," Harte said in his jumpy voice. "Wonder why he'd do that?"

"Because he remembers who helped put him in office, that's why." Munroe was a shade put out because Harte seemed so unimpressed by Munroe's influence with the Governor.

"Let's lay it right on the table, Carleton. You're in the kind of trouble that can be a real liability to the party. If that Ellison kid can prove his charges—"

"Is that why the Mayor has been avoiding me?" Munroe broke in. "Because he's afraid I'm going to become a political dead weight? I can't believe that! Not after all the years I've put in for the party—and for Mayor Arch Norwall."

"Politics is a funny business, Carleton."

"Not that funny. The Governor wasn't afraid to ask my advice and to take my committee-appointee suggestion."

"Well, let's kick that around a little. I assume two of the people on the committee will be his own men."

"Not Sylvestro."

"Dom Sylvestro from Brewer County? Mr. Honesty?

He's on the committee?" Harte sounded surprised. "Do you know who the other one is?"

"Jimmy Alexander. He's going to be chairman."

Harte chuckled. "Clever. Don't you get the picture, Carleton?"

"Maybe I'm getting dense in my old age."

"Sylvestro is from the opposition party, and you couldn't buy him with the crown jewels of England. I'm assumed to be a Munroe man. So there are the two sides of it. The deciding vote in a showdown will be Jimmy Alexander. And he'll swing toward the side with the biggest hammer."

"Which makes the whole thing a duel between me and the Governor."

"Sure, Carleton. And he was smart to put one of your own people on his committee, wasn't he? Whatever happens, you can never claim that he rolled over you."

"I'm beginning to think the whole world is rolling over me, Sid."

"Pull yourself together. The party needs you."

"Why hasn't Arch Norwall been in touch with me then?"

"He's playing it safe, Carleton. You know Arch. One of the great fence-sitting mayors of our time."

"Maybe the party needs me, Sid, but that's not quite enough to let me sleep well."

"What's the problem?"

"I'm not sure the Governor thinks he needs me."

In the few days that remained before the opening of hearings by the Governor's Special Investigating Committee, several interesting things happened.

Walter Wallace offered to hire a lawyer for his

son-in-law. Don turned him down flat. "This isn't a trial. It's a hearing. All I have to do is tell the truth."

"This is a politically arranged hearing set up to investigate politics." Wallace pointed out. "The truth may find itself out in the courthouse alley."

But Don stuck to his determination to go it alone, armed only with his little notebook.

On Thursday, the week before the hearings were to begin, Charlie Pegler called Don into his glass cubicle. "You're going to get some time off. Give you a chance to get yourself ready for the hearings. As of tomorrow, you're on leave of absence with pay."

Don met his gaze. "I wondered how long it would take."

"How long what would take?"

"How long it would take to get me out of here."

"You're not fired, Don." Charlie Pegler felt a flicker of anger. This boy had managed to mess up the voluntary-contribution arrangement and get an investigation underway.

"You're not fired," he repeated in a calmer voice. "It's just not in the department's best interest to have you here until—well, until the thing is resolved. Look, I think they're being generous downstairs. You'll be paid just as if you were here."

As Don walked back to his table, Pegler stared into the drafting room for a long time. He knew they were giving the kid the treatment out there. Nobody talked to him except in the line of work. All of his buddies had dumped him, even Barber. Funny. The kid was the only one who had stuck to his guns for everybody's benefit, and now everybody hated him for it. Guilty consciences, Pegler decided. You don't want to hang around with a guy who has proved how weak you are.

He shook his head slowly and reached for his phone. "Mr. Munroe, Ellison will be out of here as of closing time this afternoon. Like you told me."

It was done. The Man Downstairs had managed to get one benefit out of the Governor's investigation already. It had supplied him with the excuse to get rid of Ellison gracefully. The boy didn't know it, of course, but Pegler knew that at the end of the month there would be a news release stating that the department was conducting an economy drive, and that, therefore, some personnel areas would have to be cut back. Don Ellison would receive a notice in the mail; then the biweekly checks would stop coming.

Also on Thursday, Millbury Patrolman John Mangrum was called into Chief Glen Stone's office "Johnny," Stone said, his bulldog face wearing a frown, "we need somebody to represent the department at the Law Enforcement Conference in Phoenix next week. I know this comes as a surprise, but I've decided to send you out there."

Mangrum's lean cheeks bunched into a grin. He was a long-muscled young man, like a track miler. His uniform fit perfectly. Not a wrinkle. He was all spit and polish and efficiency. He'd been a Marine lieutenant, and it still showed. "I'd like that very much, sir."

Stone held back a question he wanted to ask. But if Mangrum had gotten a subpoena from the Governor's committee, surely he would have told Stone.

"You'll leave tonight, then. Take the opportunity to get a little rest, look around Arizona. Don't be too available, you know what I mean?"

"Yes, sir. I know exactly what you mean."

Stone wished Mangrum hadn't been quite so precise

about that. After the young officer had left his office, Chief Stone dialed Munroe.

"Carleton, it's done. He'll be out of reach all next week."

"I don't see how the hearing can last any longer than that," Munroe said. "Thanks, Glen. Give my best to your wife."

"Sure will, Carleton." Stone hung up, thinking that Munroe had sounded much more like his old self.

Across Millbury, The Man Downstairs thought the same thing. He'd had a few bad days, but now he was getting back his grip. Ellison was out of the department. The fact that the boy was still getting paid—for a while—was beside the point. He wasn't up there at his drafting table. The empty stool was a reminder to everyone in the room that it didn't pay to buck the system. An object lesson—that was the kind of leadership Carleton Munroe believed in.

CHAPTER 14

MILLBURY had no television station, and it took Channel 6 over in Centerham quite a while to discover that something big was going on in Millbury. The problem at Channel 6 was that the station was a small one, and the news director had been an engineer before he was made head of the news department. A week ago, the mobile unit had developed a whole potful of glitches. The news director had spent most of the week in the van with the engineer and a soldering iron. The Millbury story had gotten on the air as a thirty-second item read off the state-news wire printout. But the anchorman was more concerned with his smile and his hair than with the news he read off the long yellow sheet. Not until the Thursday evening before the hearings did the news director himself wander over to the state Teletype, wiping his hands on a rag.

"Well, the blasted mobile unit is ready to go. Finally!" he said to no one in particular, looking at the chattering Teletype as he spoke. Then he tossed the rag aside and grabbed the yellow strip that spewed from the machine.

"Holy Moley! Why hasn't anybody picked up on this? Krafke! Read this. Get what you can from the Governor's PR aide, then rush your smiling face down to Millbury with a cameraman tomorrow and interview this Ellison kid. I want something solid for tomorrow's six-o'clock news."

Channel 6's feature reporter, Ray Krafke, had a pointed face that always seemed on the verge of asking a question. His sand-colored eyebrows were permanently raised, creasing his freckled forehead. His hair was always churned into a reddish crest, even when he appeared on camera. It was his on-air trademark. The station's anchorman was a slick buttoned-down guy with beautiful "dry look" hair that he worked on for ten minutes before air time, but Krafke looked like unironed laundry, and while the pretty anchorman was strictly a "rip-and-read" reporter, Krafke dug for his news. It wasn't rehashed press-wire stuff. It was fresh, lively, original Krafke material—which was why the station manager let Krafke stay on the air.

He and Marty Fleishman, the camera and sound man, rolled into Millbury around 10 A.M. Friday in the red-and-white "Channel 6 Now News" mobile unit. It took them a while to locate the Department of Streets Building and another fifteen minutes to talk Carleton Munroe into a filmed interview on the lawn behind the building, where the midmorning light was suitable for filming.

"You're not going to hang me, are you, boys?" Munroe joked, as Fleishman took a light-meter reading and tangled the meter cord in Munroe's coat buttons.

Krafke sensed that this bird had been interviewed by TV news teams before. He was a tough old city department head, and he'd been around plenty. Krafke decided to play it in a "we-were-pushed-into-this" way.

"Look, Mr. Munroe, the boss just needs a little footage on this thing to keep up with the newspapers. They're giving it a big play, so we thought we'd better not neglect it altogether."

That seemed to make the guy a little less guarded, Krafke thought. The long horse face relaxed. "Where do you want me to stand?" Munroe asked.

"Get him over in the shade," Marty Fleishman muttered under his breath as he plugged the microphone cord into his shoulder-slung tape recorder. "That bald dome of his reflects sunlight like a beacon."

"Now we'll just talk back and forth," Krafke said when he'd placed Monroe and Fleishman had lined up his camera. "At some point, Marty will start filming." He knew the camera and tape recorder were already going, but he'd found it useful not to tell his interview subjects exactly when the eyes and ears went on.

"You are Carleton J. Munroe, head of the Department of Streets here in Millbury?" Krafke moved the hand mike near Munroe's mouth.

"That's right."

"How do you feel about the Governor's Special Investigating Committee coming to Millbury?"

"I'm not worried about it."

"Not worried?" That was an interesting word choice, Krafke thought. "Are there people who are worried?" Let him chew on that.

"That isn't what I meant."

He wouldn't bite.

"Let me refresh my memory on this," Krafke said.

109

"It began when one of your employees refused to pay a voluntary contribution, I believe it's called."

Munroe picked his way through his reply like a man with heavy boots in a minefield. "We do . . . provide the, um, opportunity for our people to support the party, yes."

"And if they choose not to?"

"Ellison has been the only one."

"In all the years the voluntary-contribution plan has been in effect, Donald Ellison has been the only employee of the Department of Streets not to pay?"

"Not to contribute," Munroe corrected him.

"And what has happened to him?"

"Happened?"

Cagey old bureaucrat, Krafke thought. "Yes, because he didn't contribute."

"Nothing has happened to him."

"Yet we have been told that he isn't here." Was that sweat beginning to film Munroe's sloping forehead?

"He has been given a leave of absence until the hearings are over."

"At his own request and with pay?"

"Yes, with pay."

"But he didn't ask for the leave?"

Munroe was definitely uncomfortable. "I thought it best in view of the circumstances."

"How long is this leave of absence?"

"Indefinite."

Aha! "But you just stated that it was only until the hearings are over."

"I did? Well, strike that. In fact, strike all the comment about Ellison's leave."

Krafke smiled. He would ignore the request. He'd found the weak spot. "You said—at least I have the definite impression that you said Ellison has been suspended."

"Not suspended as such."

"But he's not here."

"He has been given leave with pay," Munroe snapped.

"When will he return?"

"No date has been set."

"The committee hearing is expected to last no longer than a few days. Isn't it possible that Ellison will be back on the job within a week or so?"

Munroe glared at him. "No comment."

Nice, Krafke thought. Nice. Couldn't have written it better myself. "Thank you, Mr. Carleton Munroe," he said into the mike. "This is Ray Krafke, downstate in Millbury for Channel Six Now News."

He and Fleishman pulled into the parking lot near Don and Sue's apartment a few minutes before noon. It took Krafke almost twenty minutes to convince Don that he had nothing to lose by being interviewed. "Right here in the kitchen," he told Fleishman. "Go get your lights."

He had a couple of reasons for this. One was that a little knot of people had gathered out front, and he didn't need any kibitzing from a crowd. Another reason was that the kid was so nervous that Krafke figured he'd feel more secure in his own kitchen. Besides, kitchen interviews had a solid, homey look on the air.

Sue began to clear the table. "No, leave the cups there, if you will, Mrs. Ellison. I'd like this to look just like what it is—a conversation over morning coffee, okay?"

They sat at the small kitchen table, all three of them.

The wife will be a nice touch, Krafke figured. Cute as a kitten, too.

"I'm here in the Millbury apartment of Don and Sue Ellison. Don is the Department of Streets employee who refused to make a political contribution, and that refusal has led to the Governor's Special Investigating Committee hearing that is to begin Monday. Now, Don—" The kid was too young to be called "Mr. Ellison," and Krafke liked the first-name approach for this particular interview. "Don, you claim that the contribution is not voluntary."

"That's right, sir."

Krafke was pleased with the "sir." It made the kid seem as sincere as sunlight.

"I understand that you are on a leave of absence from the Department of Streets."

"That's right."

"With pay?"

"Yes, sir."

"For how long?"

"I'm on leave until the hearing is over, I guess."

"Aren't you aware that apparently no time limit has been set on this leave of absence?"

"That isn't what Mr. Pegler told me."

"Who is Pegler?"

"The department's chief engineer. He told me it was just until the hearing is over." The boy's eyes told Krafke that was the truth. Very interesting.

"Mr. Munroe's version was different. In fact, he refused to comment when I asked him for a time limit on your suspension."

"Leave of absence."

Krafke's pointed nose twitched, something that

happened involuntarily when he'd stumbled onto a story that got better as he probed into it.

"You don't agree, then, that you may already have been dismissed by the Department of Streets?"

"No. I'm on a leave of absence with pay until the hearing is over. That's the way Mr. Pegler explained it to me."

"Thank you, Don Ellison." He turned toward the camera. "This is Ray Krafke, Channel Six Now News, in Millbury."

On the return trip to Centerham, he said to Fleishman, "You realize that when I edit this stuff, I can intercut Munroe with Ellison and make Munroe sound like one of the world's biggest liars?"

Fleishman's little round head nodded, but he didn't take his eyes off the road. "Now you wouldn't do a thing like that, would you, boss?"

Krafke matched Fleishman's grin with a rare grin of his own. "Sure, I would."

CHAPTER 15

At six thirty Friday evening, State Senator Dominic Sylvestro settled back in a plastic webbed reclining chair on the patio of his upstate cattle farm. Leona, his wife, was finishing the dishes in the kitchen, and he could hear the faint clinks as she dried and stacked them in the cupboard over the sink. Senator Sylvestro's two teen-aged daughters were out in the barn, helping the herdsman to bed down eighteen head of prize black angus.

This was the senator's "quiet hour." None of the family would interrupt the solid hour of TV news he was about to watch; first the local coverage from Channel 6, then the national network news. He folded his hands on his flat stomach and waited out the sign-on and the commercials.

Senator Sylvestro was a compact man; he had a tendency to put on weight if he didn't watch his diet. His dark complexion gave him a look of deep suntan the year round. His heavy black hair, combed in deep waves, was just beginning to show a distinguished sparkle of silver.

The opening story brought Sylvestro to full attention. The anchorman offered a one-minute update on the Millbury thing; then Ray Krafke's foxy face came on camera. Sylvestro didn't like Krafke. He didn't know anyone in the State Legislature who did. Krafke was a little too eager to back you into corners. But you did have to give the man credit for knowing his trade. He was a darned accurate and thorough newsman.

"Today, Now News traveled to Millbury, where a hearing on alleged macing in the Department of Streets will begin to unfold on Monday. I interviewed Carleton Munroe, head of that department, and I also talked with Donald Ellison, the young Department of Streets employee who has refused to make a political contribution, and who now appears to be out of a job because of that refusal. Mr. Munroe seems confident, however, that the hearing will not be damaging to his department."

The scene jumped to film footage of Carleton Munroe standing on the lawn outside the Department of Streets Building. "I'm not worried about it," he said.

Krafke ran true to form, leading Munroe on with seemingly innocent questions. They got to the subject of Donald Ellison's job status.

Krafke: "How long is this leave of absence?"

Munroe: "Indefinite."

"That isn't the way Don Ellison sees it," said Krafke's voice off camera as Ellison appeared on the screen, sitting in his kitchen. Sylvestro was surprised at how young he looked.

Ellison: "I'm on leave until the hearing is over, I guess."

Krafke: "Aren't you aware that apparently no time limit has been set?"

Ellison: "That isn't what Mr. Pegler told me."

Krafke: "Who is Pegler?"

Ellison: "The department's chief engineer. He told me it was just until the hearing is over."

Munroe was back. "When will he return?" asked Krafke's voice off camera.

Munroe: "No date has been set."

There was more, but Senator Sylvestro was already lifting the receiver of his patio phone. He dialed his legislative aide at her home in Centerham. "Peggy, I want you to track down Carleton Munroe in Millbury and ask him to call me here at the farm. I'll be available all evening."

The phone rang twelve minutes later. "Senator Sylvestro? This is Carleton Munroe."

"Did you see the coverage on Channel Six?"

"Yes, I did." Munroe's voice was wary.

"Is Krafke on the right track? Is that boy fired?"

"Senator, you know how TV reporters are. They could edit the Bible so Moses would look bad."

"I asked you a straight question, Munroe. Is that boy fired?"

"He's still on the payroll."

"For how long?"

Munroe hesitated. "Well, don't you think that should be determined by the outcome of the hearing, Senator?"

Not a bad answer. Sylvestro's estimation of Munroe went up a notch from rock bottom. "It sounded on television very much as if you had already made up your mind about the outcome, Munroe."

"I'm sorry if you got that impression, Senator. If they had shown the whole interview in one piece from the beginning, maybe you—"

"Munroe," Sylvestro interrupted, "I'm known for fairness and honesty in the State Senate. I look for that in every man. I don't think it's too much to hope for. When I see unfairness and dishonesty, especially when I see it in positions of public trust, it infuriates me. Will you bear that in mind, Munroe?"

"Of course, Senator. I know your reputation well, and I admire it. Will that be all, Senator?"

Sylvestro grimaced at the phone. "For now, yes. I presume we will have more to say next week." He hung up and tried to concentrate on TV again. That Munroe was hard to read. A cool one, a really cool one.

Down in Millbury, the cool one was sweating.

"Yes, I'll have another coffee," Hobie Hasfeld boomed on Saturday night, "if somebody will just ask me."

"I'm sorry, Hobie," Sue said. She stood up from the kitchen table, took the pot from the stove where she had been keeping it warm, and poured the big reporter a second cup. "I just don't feel like talking tonight."

"Neither of you does." Hobie forced a grin. "I thought the hearing was what we all wanted."

Don looked up from the spoon he had been toying with. "I had a dream last night. I was on the witness stand and the judge asked me something. I don't remember what. But I couldn't think of an answer. I just sat there paralyzed, and everybody in the courtroom stared at me, waiting—just stared without making a sound. Then somebody dropped something, and when I woke up—"

"Oh," Sue broke in. "That must have been when I knocked my book off the night table."

"When I woke up, I was in a cold sweat. And I was even more scared than when I'd been dreaming. What am I doing in this mess?"

"Steady there, old buddy of the oppressed and downtrodden. It's never easy to stick up for what you think is right, remember? Anyway, your dream is a lot of stuff. The hearing isn't in a courtroom, you won't be in a witness box, and there's no judge."

"I just wish it was over."

"The way that TV reporter talked, you'd better hope it stretches out. You could be out of work when it ends."

"That's not how Charlie Pegler talked," Don insisted.

"So you said."

"So he said."

"But he's not the head guy."

"Oh, stop it!" Sue put in. "I'm so tired of all this!"

Hobie scowled at her. "Come on, kid. Don's holding up pretty well, considering he's the guy who laid himself on the line. He needs you up on the front, not sneaking back to rest camp."

She nodded her head. "I know it. I know it, Hobie. I'm sorry. It's just that I keep thinking back to how simple everything seemed before all this happened."

"Everybody feels that way when something goes wrong, Sue. Nothing to be ashamed of."

Don toyed with the spoon again, twisting it around and around with his thumb and forefinger. "I wonder how I'll do at the hearing. I've never been in front of a big crowd like that before."

"How about that time you played in *Oklahoma?* "

"That was a bit part in a school play, Hobie. I had the whole class on stage with me. And the audience was pulling for us all the way."

Hobie wrapped his thick fingers around his cup and took a long drag of coffee. "You'll do all right," he said. But deep down, he suddenly wasn't all that sure.

On Sunday morning, Calvin Ellison glanced sideways at his wife, who still knelt, still prayed, though they had been in the church pew a full five minutes. She was praying for their son, for Don. On the way to church Mildred Ellison had told Calvin she was going to do that.

"I'm not so sure the Lord will be concerned with Don's kind of problem," he had replied as he pulled their old Chevy into the church parking lot.

"The Lord is interested in everyone," she said. Her tone told him that was all there was to it. She was going to pray for Don, period.

So be it, then. If her little prayer could help the boy any, what was the harm? He slid back against the hard pew. This was her kind of church, one in which you were purposely made uncomfortable, as if discomfort would bring you closer to God. He wasn't altogether sure he'd be here at all if Mildred weren't such a churchgoer. He felt closer to Heaven when he plowed a field with the tractor roaring under him and smelled God's rich earth as the plowshare rolled it over to grow warm in the spring air. The open fields were his church.

He studied Mildred's thin back, still bent over her folded hands. There sure couldn't be any harm in a

119

little extra shot at it, he decided. He shut his eyes. *If you've got a spare minute or two next week, Lord, you might look in on our boy. I suspect he's going to need all the help he can get.*

Mildred sighed and sat back. With a quick turn of her head, she caught his eye. He nodded, and he knew that she gathered right away what he had done, because she smiled.

Down in Millbury, the white-haired court-building custodian muttered to himself as he lined up the chairs in Hearing Room 2A and placed pads and pencils on the committee table.

"Lotta nonsense, this one. Been kickbacks long's I can remember." He nudged a chair into line with his shoe.

"Not just in the Department of Streets, no, sirree. Republicans, Democrats, all the same. Lotta foolishness, this hearing. Lotta rumbling and mumbling." He picked up his push broom and jabbed at some invisible dust in a corner. He was a short, bow-legged man—nobody knew how old—who wore a white shirt and a black bow tie no matter what sort of work he was doing.

"Fumbling and bumbling." He liked the sound of that. He really could have been a songwriter if he'd set his mind to it when he was younger, he thought,

> Rumbling and mumbling,
> Fumbling and bumbling,
> That's the way the world is run,
> That's the way that things are done,
> Right here in Millbury City.

He chuckled. Not bad. "Rumbling and mumbling . . ." He experimented with a tune for it, his whistle sounding thin in the big empty room.

He'd seen a lot of hearings, and this one wasn't going to be much different, he thought. A good old whitewash for the city. That's what it would be, all right. Only thing that bothered him was how young that Ellison was. He'd seen him on the TV the other night. Seemed like a nice kid, too nice to get torn to pieces in here.

He shrugged and wet his lips. The whistle was sharp and tuneless.

> That's the way that things are done,
> Right here in Millbury City. . . .

CHAPTER 16

THE GAVEL slammed down, and Hearing Room 2A quieted. The sharp rap took Don by surprise, and he jumped in his chair.

"The Governor's Special Committee on Alleged Political Malpractices in the City of Millbury is now in session," State Senator James Alexander announced into his table microphone. Then he proceeded to take the edge off his dramatic moment with a long-winded speech. "We are here today," he began, "to determine the depth, accuracy, and seriousness of the charges brought about by an employee of a city department through the medium of several newspapers stories. . . ."

Alexander's voice rumbled on. He was a tall man, lean as a heron. With his pinstripe blue suit and fluffy silver hair, he looked more like a British diplomat than an automobile dealer from Centerham. He was quite a contrast to the other two men on his committee.

State Senator Dominic Sylvestro had sunk deeper in

his chair as he realized that Alexander's opening remarks were going to be long ones. He made a tent of his fingers and bounced them against his mouth. To Don, he looked like a prizefighter who hadn't yet had his face flattened. His dark eyes swept over the room, met Don's gaze, and held it.

Don shifted his study to the committee member at Alexander's left. Sid Harte was a lot fatter than he'd looked on the posters Don had tacked up along Country Boulevard. And he'd let his frizzy brown hair grow until it covered his ears. Harte's green blazer and emerald tie were a noisy contrast to Sylvestro's quiet beige suit. Chairman Alexander may not look like a car dealer, Don thought, but Sid Harte sure looks like the owner of a hole-in-the-wall bar and grill. Which he was.

The three committee members sat behind the center of a long table placed across the front of the room. They were flanked at the table by assorted aides and clerks and a grim-looking court stenographer in dark gray, who tapped out every word of Alexander's speech on her little black box.

In front of the committee table was another, much smaller table with three chairs facing the committee. They were empty for the moment, but Don knew with a knot in his stomach that that was where the witnesses would sit as the committee fired its questions.

Rows of upholstered theaterlike chairs filled the rest of the room. The first two rows on the right side were reserved for members of the press, although television coverage had been barred as too disruptive. The press seats were filled. In his seat along the wall, Hobie Hasfeld turned, caught Don's eye, and gave him a little twist of a smile. Good old Hobie. Great old Hobie! He'd gotten Don into this mess.

123

No. that wasn't fair. Don had decided to make a fight of it, and here was where the fight was to take place. Would he have the nerve to see it through?

Don sat in the front row on the left, where he'd been asked to sit by the hearing-room usher. Sue was beside him and next to her, grim-faced and probably as nervous as he was, slumped Gil Barber, Kent Watters, and Eddie Koslowski. Somewhere in the crowded room was The Man Downstairs. The usher wouldn't dare tell *him* where to sit.

Chairman Alexander's drone stopped. The hearing room held its breath. He poured a glass of water from the green plastic pitcher in front of him. He drank slowly, put the glass down with a clunk, cleared his throat.

"The Chair calls Mayor Archibald Norwall."

In the center of the room, Arch Norwall rose and strode to the witness table. He was a tall, weatherbeaten man with a jumpy Adam's apple. His large ears stuck out beneath thin gray hair carefully combed across a large bald spot.

He was sworn in by a court clerk who scurried around the end of the committee table, held out a Bible for Norwall's left hand, then scurried back. The Mayor sat down.

"I'd like to dispense with formality long enough to say good morning, Mr. Mayor," Alexander said pleasantly. "The Mayor is an old friend of mine."

Don groaned inwardly. If this was going to be old-home week among political cronies, what chance would he have up there?

"Now, Mayor Norwall, the committee would like your opinion on alleged pressure put upon city employees to force them to contribute money for political purposes. Is there such pressure?"

Norwall cleared his throat. Twice. The ragged sound, amplified by the witness-table microphone, bounced around the room. "I wouldn't call it pressure, Mr. Chairman. It's more of an opportunity to support the party. Our loyal employees have always taken advantage of that opportunity."

"Is this practice city-wide?"

"The support? Yes."

"I meant the opportunity to provide that support, Arch— Mayor Norwall."

"You mean are all city departments given a chance to contribute? Yes."

"How?"

Norwall looked puzzled. "How what?"

"How are the departments told of this chance to support the party?" Alexander said.

"It's understood."

"The department heads just know what's to be done?"

"They know contributions are sought before each election, yes."

Alexander seemed satisfied. He looked left and right at his committee members. "Any questions from you gentlemen?"

Sid Harte shook his head. You bet, Don thought. The city councilman sure wasn't going to question his own mayor.

"I have a question," Senator Sylvestro said unexpectedly in his high, thin voice. "Mayor Norwall, how much pressure is put upon a city employee who chooses not to contribute?"

"Pressure? I'm not sure I know what you mean."

"I mean is there any record of anyone having been fired because he or she refused to contribute?"

"No," the Mayor said. "There is no record of that." His voice was steady, but Don noticed that his ears had turned pink.

Sylvestro smiled. "There may be no record, at that," he said almost to himself. "Let me rephrase that question. Has anyone ever been fired for that reason?"

"Not to my knowledge."

"It's possible, though, that a department head may have fired people that you aren't aware of, isn't it?"

Norwall considered that for a moment. "I can't possibly keep completely up to date on the day-to-day business of every department. That's why I have department heads."

"Uh-huh," Senator Sylvestro grunted.

Chairman Alexander glared at him. "If there are no more questions," Alexander said, "you are excused, Mayor Norwall. The committee thanks you for your cooperation."

Hobie turned in his seat and rolled his eyes in an expression of frustration. Don nodded grimly.

The next witnesses were a parade of colorless city officials connected with the Mayor's office, each of them swearing that contributions were always voluntary—though, of course, there may have been an overzealous department head here and there. None of them, they said, had ever heard of anyone being fired for refusing to contribute.

Then the hearing broke for lunch. Hobie pushed through the crowd to join Don and Sue. The three of them walked across the street to a sandwich shop.

"So far, it's been a whitewash," Hobie said between bites of grilled cheese, "a big word play, and Alexander is letting them get away with it."

"How about Sylvestro, though? He puts his two cents in now and then," Don pointed out.

"He's our big hope. He hasn't really said much so far, but I think that's because he doesn't want to antagonize the rest of the committee this early."

The hearing resumed at two. A sharp rap of the gavel, and Alexander's rumbly voice called, "Edward Koslowski."

Eddie's light hair had been slicked down for once. His maroon tie was in place, and he was neater than usual. But he'd lost weight, and his seersucker suit seemed to hang on him.

To Don's surprise, a stocky middle-aged man in an expensive blue suit arose from the audience and followed Eddie to the witness table. His sculptured black hair and the careful fit of his clothes didn't tell Don anything. The tip-off was the briefcase.

"Who's that?" Sue whispered.

"I think Eddie's got himself a lawyer."

The chairman said, "You are Edward Koslowski?"

Eddie nodded.

"And this other gentleman?"

"Attorney George Franklin," the fashion plate said smoothly into the microphone in front of his chair. "I have been retained to represent Mr. Koslowski, Mr. Watters, and Mr. Barber."

A murmur swept the room. What was expected to be routine information seeking now promised to become a more serious game.

"All three are your clients, Mr. Franklin?"

127

"That is correct, Mr. Chairman."

"Who specifically retained you?" Senator Sylvestro broke in.

"You're out of order, Senator," the Chairman growled at him. "But you may answer the question, Mr. Franklin."

"I'm afraid that happens to be privileged information between client and counsel, Mr. Chairman."

Alexander scowled. "The clerk will proceed with the swearing in."

"Now, Mr. Koslowski," he resumed after Eddie was seated, "how long have you worked for the Department of Streets?"

"Eleven years."

"You are certainly familiar, then, with Department of Streets procedures?"

"Yes, sir."

"Is it standard department procedure to ask each employee to make political contributions?"

Eddie covered his mike with his hand and whispered to the lawyer, who covered his own mike and whispered back.

"It's a standard procedure to suggest it," he said.

"How is that suggestion made?"

"By memo."

"To each employee?"

"Yes." The lawyer leaned over and whispered. Eddie added, "The same mimeographed memo to each employee."

"If I may, Mr. Chairman," Franklin said, "I happen to have a copy of the memo with me."

Don squirmed in his chair. Maybe he'd made a mistake in turning down Walter Wallace's offer of a lawyer of his own . . .

No. Not if he was determined to see this through himself. Truth was truth, and he thought that was all he would need up there.

Franklin pulled from his briefcase a clean, unfolded sheet of paper.

"Read it, please," Alexander ordered.

In a voice that would have put Walter Cronkite to shame, the lawyer read the memo that had started the whole chain of events leading to this hearing room.

"I respectfully ask the Chair to note," Franklin added, "that nowhere in that memo is there any threat or implication of a threat of any kind."

"So noted."

The committee then asked Eddie a few questions about his own contributions, and Eddie came out of it as a loyal city employee, confused and disturbed about this big fuss.

Kent Watters was called. As he passed Eddie in the aisle, Don was sure Eddie gave him a quick wink. Franklin stayed at the witness table.

The questioning of Watters was a carbon copy of Eddie's appearance. Kent added nothing as he echoed Eddie's testimony. Chairman Alexander appeared satisfied and dismissed him. Attorney Franklin smiled, and Don was miserable.

"The Chair calls Gilbert Barber."

Gil almost leaped out of his seat and trotted to the witness table. He was sworn in and sat down grinning at Franklin. Don wondered how many sessions the lawyer had held with all three of them to get their stories straight. There was no doubt in Don's mind about who had hired Franklin. The whole thing was typical of behind-the-scenes maneuvers by The Man Downstairs.

The questions aimed at Gil were the same as those

129

asked Eddie, and Kent. Gil answered in the same "who-me-make-trouble?" way, and he sneaked a self-satisfied look over his shoulder at the audience.

Then Senator Sylvestro dropped a bomb. "With the Chair's permission," he said, "I'd like to ask you, Mr. Barber, what happened to the resistance you tried to organize in July against payment of the contribution."

A gasp of surprise rippled through the room. Gil's smug smile dissolved.

"Looks like Sylvestro has his own information pipeline," Don whispered to Sue. She nodded glumly, and Don knew she didn't like any of this.

At the witness table, Gil licked dry lips. Franklin bent sideways to mutter in Gil's ear, hand over his mike. "Uh," Gil said, "that was . . . that was . . ."

Franklin was whispering again. Gil shook his head. Franklin's face clouded, and he appeared to insist on making his point.

"That was just talk," Gil finally got out.

"Talk?"

"Like, you know, I got talking and, well, I guess I was sort of showing off."

"In other words," Sylvestro pressed, "you were talking to impress your friends?"

Gil sank back in his chair. "I guess you could put it that way."

"Then I take it that resistance to the contribution was—and is—a daring action."

"I object!" Franklin shouted.

Chairman Alexander gazed at him with a half-smile. "This isn't a trial, Counselor. We are simply seeking information."

Franklin twisted in his chair, red-faced.

"You may answer the question, Mr. Barber."

130

Gil looked confused. "What was the question?"

"The question is," Sylvestro said patiently, "is it considered daring to withhold your contribution?"

"I didn't withhold it."

"Come on now, Mr. Barber, don't play word games with this committee. Is it possible to refuse to make a contribution without fear of some sort of punishment?"

Franklin whispered.

Gil spoke quickly. "I don't know of a single specific case where an employee refused to pay and was punished for it."

"That wasn't Gil talking," Don told Sue. "That was Franklin."

"The witness is excused," Alexander said wearily. "Call Mr. William Crimm."

Billy Crimm lumbered out of the audience, his paunch bouncing as he strode down the sloped center aisle. The slick hair glistened on his bullet head under the ceiling lights. He was sworn in. The witness chair creaked as he sat down and nodded at George Franklin. The lawyer apparently represented Billy Crimm, too!

"You are an employee of the Department of Streets, Mr. Crimm?"

"Seventeen years, sir."

"Frankly, I have no questions for you," Chairman Alexander said. "Senator Sylvestro asked that you be called. Senator?"

"Mr. Crimm, what is your specific assignment in the department's drafting room?"

"In charge of survey books."

"What are survey books?"

"Notebooks the survey crews keep in the field. Rod readings, topography notes."

"You file these books?"

"Yes, sir. And compute elevations for cross-section sheets."

"Isn't that simply subtraction of the survey-rod readings from the benchmark elevations? Simple arithmetic?"

Crimm squinted at him, and Franklin seemed puzzled. "It's not calculus," Crimm said, and the audience gave him the laugh he was looking for.

"That doesn't seem like a very demanding job after seventeen years, Mr. Crimm. What other responsibilities do you have?"

Billy frowned. "Other responsibilities?"

"Come on, Crimm." Sylvestro's voice was like a blade. "Are you not a personal assistant to Mr. Munroe?"

Franklin whispered.

"We all assist Mr. Munroe." Billy's voice had dried out and came in a harsh rasp. A shiver raced along Don's back. There was something familiar about that gravelly voice.

Sid Harte spoke up for the first time this afternoon. "I object to the Senator's attempt to make Mr. Crimm into—"

"I'm not attempting to make him into anything," Sylvestro rapped back. "I know exactly what he is and I—"

"Mr. Chairman," Harte protested, "will you remind the Senator that he is to address the Chair, not me directly?"

"Gentlemen, gentlemen!" Alexander tapped his gavel. "This has gone far enough."

"No, it hasn't," Sylvestro said. "I call upon Mr. Crimm to admit that he is in the drafting room primarily to report to Mr. Munroe."

"A lie!" The amplifying system rattled. Billy had risen half out of his chair. "That's a lie!"

And then Don recognized the hoarse rasp. "Sue! Those midnight calls—he was the one on the phone! Billy Crimm!"

Sue was wide-eyed. "And that call about the accident—that was the same voice. I'm sure of it!"

The gavel slammed down and the room quieted.

"I ask you," Sylvestro persisted, "do you or do you not report directly to Mr. Munroe?"

Billy looked at Franklin. The lawyer sat tight-lipped, staring at the wall behind the committee table. Crimm poured a glass of water with shaking hands and spilled some of it on his tie.

"Mr. Crimm?"

"I do have—uh, some direct contact with Mr. Munroe."

Sylvestro leaned forward. "In effect, you are his spy in the drafting room. Is that an accurate statement?"

Crimm stared at him. Then he nodded. The audience gasped.

Where was Sylvestro getting his information? Somebody had to be feeding the Senator the facts, somebody Don had never suspected was on his side. Don had never quite trusted Billy Crimm, but somebody else knew exactly what Crimm was.

Sylvestro wasn't finished yet. "Now that we've established your true status, Mr. Crimm, I'd like to know whether or not you reported to Mr. Munroe that Mr. Koslowski, Mr. Watters, Mr. Barber, and Mr. Ellison at any time threatened to withhold their contribution."

Crimm was a beaten man. He ran a hand over his

133

slick hair and left it rumpled in a rooster comb. "I—I did report that to Mr. Munroe, yes."

"Then it is true," Sylvestro shouted above the rising mutter from the audience, "it is true that Mr. Munroe wanted to be made aware of anyone who refused to pay?"

Crimm twisted like a trapped animal.

"Mr. Crimm, answer the question!" Chairman Alexander ordered.

Crimm broke. "Yes! Yes, it's true!"

The gavel slammed, and Alexander shouted, "This hearing is adjourned until tomorrow morning at nine."

CHAPTER 17

ON THIS second day of the hearing, Don took his seat with the empty feeling that he wanted to be called only so he could get it over with. That's no good, he told himself angrily. You started this thing, now see it through.

He felt tired and dragged out, though yesterday he hadn't done anything but sit here. Funny how mental strain alone could wear you down. Beside him, Sue looked fresh and bouncy in her light-green pantsuit, but there were shadows under her eyes, too. They'd had a restless night, even though yesterday afternoon Hobie had tried to make things sound much better than Don suspected they were.

"Sylvestro definitely knows what's going on," he'd told them over a wagon-wheel-sized pizza they'd shared in the Italian place on Mill Street. "Looks like he's got his own source of information in the department. Question is, will the other two on the committee let him run free, or are they going to try to block him?"

Now the committee filed in, and Alexander rapped the gavel hard three times. The room quieted.

"Good morning, ladies and gentlemen," he said pleasantly. "The hearing is back in session." He consulted a paper on the table. "The Chair calls Donald Ellison."

This soon? Don hadn't expected to be up there for another whole day! He rose on wavering legs and walked past Koslowski, Watters, and Gil Barber without looking at them. He wasn't snubbing the three, but after yesterday he didn't know how to behave toward them.

The leather-covered Bible felt pebbly under his damp fingers. He repeated what the clerk said, then sat alone at the witness table. He wondered if Attorney George Franklin with his sculptured hair was back there in the crowd waiting for Don to hang himself.

"You are Donald Ellison?"

"Yes, sir."

"And how long have you been employed by the Department of Streets?"

"Just under eight months."

"In what capacity?"

"As a draftsman." His voice seemed tiny in this big room.

"Would you speak into the microphone, please?"

Don pulled the table mike closer. "As a draftsman," he repeated. This time his amplified voice startled him.

"Now, Mr. Ellison," Chairman Alexander began in a fatherly tone, "according to statements you made to the *Millbury Chronicle,* statements also carried on the news wires, you were allegedly threatened with the loss of your job if you refused to contribute as requested in the memo we reviewed yesterday."

136

"That's right."

"Do you have any proof of such a threat?"

Don hesitated. "Proof? You mean something written down?"

"Documentary evidence, yes."

"It was all done by conversation."

Sid Harte looked relieved. Senator Sylvestro scowled. Chairman Alexander seemed neutral. "Conversation with whom?"

"With—" Don almost said Charlie Pegler, but that wasn't fair. Pegler had been only the messenger. "With Mr. Munroe."

The room buzzed.

"Carleton Munroe actually threatened you with the loss of your job if you didn't contribute?"

"That's right."

"When?"

Don reached into his sports jacket and came out with the notebook. He flipped it open, turned a page. Ten days ago."

"Were there others present?"

"No, we were alone in his office." A trickle of perspiration ran down Don's left side.

"So this is a matter of your word against his?"

Don was silent. Hobie had warned him that the committee would say he lacked solid evidence.

"Questions, gentlemen?" Alexander glanced at his committee members.

"I have a question," Sid Harte offered. "Do you realize, Mr. Ellison, that you are sitting here damaging the reputation of a civil servant who has contributed most of his life to the City of Millbury?"

"I object to that!" Senator Sylvestro snapped. "It's not a question; it's a statement of opinion."

Alexander nodded. "I tend to agree. Councilman Harte, please confine yourself to direct questions without editorials."

Harte seemed deflated. "No further questions."

Don was stunned. Was this going to be it? Was this how the big issue was to be settled, in a fuzzy cat-and-mouse game between committee members?

"Mr. Chairman," he said urgently.

Alexander faced him. "You want to address the Chair?"

"I . . . guess so." Don wasn't sure of the proper procedure. "There's more to say. I just don't think—"

Alexander bristled. "The committee will conduct this hearing as it sees fit, Mr. Ellison. Are you actually questioning the—"

"Wait a minute, wait a minute!" Senator Sylvestro burst into his mike.

The gavel slammed. "You are out of order, Senator!"

"Are we after facts here, or aren't we?" Sylvestro persisted. "Do we want to hear what these witnesses have to say, or don't we?"

Alexander studied him for a long, silent moment. "Well, I was going to get to you next, Senator. You have the floor."

"And I do have some questions, since I seem to be the only member of this committee who has done his homework."

"Objection! Objection!" Sid Harte shouted.

The gavel came down again. "Yes, I object too," Alexander said icily, his face crimson. "Confine yourself to questions, Senator, not personal remarks."

"It's just that I'm getting tired of beating around bushes," Sylvestro said. Alexander began to open his mouth to speak, but Sylvestro held up a silencing hand. "Don't worry, don't worry. Questions only."

He swung toward Don. "I recall that you claimed in statements to the press that you were harassed by anonymous phone calls and by actions of the Millbury Police Department. Is that correct?"

"Yes, sir."

"Do you have any evidence of that?"

"Not of the phone calls." Hobie had told him last night that it would be useless to name Billy Crimm as the midnight caller. There was no way to prove it. "But I do have Xerox copies of the traffic tickets," Don said. That had been Hobie's idea, and he'd copied each ticket on the newspaper's machine before Don sent it in with his payment. Don pulled the sheaf of copies from his pocket. The clerk took them to Alexander, who passed them to Sylvestro.

The Senator leafed through the sheets and looked at his notes. "There were other incidents, I understand, where you were not given tickets."

"I was given some warnings along with the tickets. Finally, my wife and I were stopped by two officers with guns out, and we were searched. That was the night of July—"

"But you weren't arrested," Sid Harte interrupted.

"I have the floor," Sylvestro reminded him. "I believe you stated, Mr. Ellison, that one of the officers who detained you that night had also stopped you previously."

"Yes, sir."

"What was the reason he gave for stopping you and your wife with a drawn gun?"

"He didn't give any reason at the time. When the *Chronicle* reporter checked, the police told him they had mistaken us for a couple who had stolen a car in Clairmont."

"And you were quoted in the papers, I recall, as stating that you didn't believe this. Why not?"

"That officer knew my car. He knew my license number, and he knew me by name. Mill Street is well lighted. He had to know it was me."

"Do you have this officer's name?"

"J. Mangrum." Don flipped the pages of his notebook. "He stopped me on July twenty-seventh for going thirty-seven in a thirty-five-mile zone and on July thirty-first for what he said looked like a cracked brake-light glass. When I checked, I found that it wasn't broken."

"Do you have in that notebook a complete listing of the times you were stopped by the police?"

"Yes, sir."

"May the committee have that material?"

"Object!" Sid Harte cried. "How in the world can we tell whether or not he's simply made it all up?"

"It will be a simple matter to compare his list with the reports filed by the officers involved, won't it, Councilman?"

"If the officers actually reported each—" Harte began. Then he realized what he was saying.

"Care to complete your comment?" Alexander asked him.

Harte stared at the table in silence.

"Have you any more questions, Senator Sylvestro?"

"As a matter of fact, I have. Are you presently employed, Mr. Ellison?"

"I'm on a paid leave of absence from the Department of Streets."

"Until what date?"

"I think until this hearing is over."

"But no specific date was given you?"

"No."

"I think that's all, Mr. Chairman."

"Thank you, Mr. Ellison," Alexander said. "You are excused."

As Don walked back to his seat, the committeee went into a whispered huddle. Then Alexander rapped for order. "Apparently there has been an oversight, and no subpoena was issued for Officer Mangrum. We will adjourn until two P.M. so that this oversight can be rectified." He lifted the gavel, but a voice from the back of the room stopped it in midair.

"Mr. Chairman!"

Alexander squinted. "Who is that? Who interrupts these proceedings?"

"Chief of the Millbury Police, Glen Stone, Mr. Chairman." Heads whirled. There stood Stone in uniform, holding in both hands his white garrison cap with its gold-decorated visor.

"You wish to address the Chair, Chief Stone?"

"Yes, sir. To tell you that Officer Mangrum is representing the city at a law-enforcement conference in the West. I'm afraid he's more or less unreachable."

"I see," Alexander said, his voice hardening. "I trust you yourself will stay closer to home for the duration of the hearing, Chief." He banged the gavel. "Adjourned until two P.M. "

CHAPTER 18

THE THREE committee members lunched together in a private dining room at the Hotel Millbury Arms.

"Can't you both see that it stinks?" Senator Sylvestro demanded as their waiter left and shut the door behind him.

"I don't think we should make statements like that, Dominic, until we have some sort of proof."

"Well, I have it right here, Jimmy. Got it from the police department report sheets last week."

Sid Harte looked as if he were going to strangle on his salad. "How?"

"Just sent one of my staffers in there to do a little research."

"I can't believe it was that easy," Alexander said.

"Oh, it wasn't easy. But in the main, the Millbury Police are an honest bunch of people. And it didn't hurt a bit that I sent in a particular member of my staff. She happens to be an absolute knockout."

Harte's mouth twisted. "You sneaky—"

"Here, here!" Alexander raised a hand between them. "A little dignity, gentlemen. Dominic, just what have you got?"

"My list of incidents involving young Ellison—the list I had compiled from police files—tallies exactly with his list in this notebook. Day, time, place. Obviously they were harassing the very devil out of that boy, but most of them didn't appear to like doing it. That's why the reports are so complete, I suppose. I give Ellison great credit for standing up against that kind of treatment the way he has."

"All right," Sid Harte said around a bite of sesame roll, "so I'll grant you that the kid was stopped a few more times than you might expect."

"Why would I expect him to be stopped at all, Sid?"

"Why, he's just a kid. You know how they drive."

"He's a married man with an apartment and a respectable job, Councilman."

"All right, all right. So the police came down on him. So what does it prove?"

Senator Sylvestro dumped a spoonful of sugar into his iced tea. He stirred it slowly. "The obvious question is: on whose orders?"

"The Chair calls Chief Glen Stone."

The afternoon session got underway precisely at two. Suspense had built all through lunch. "I've got a feeling this thing's going to wind up today," Hobie had said while he, Don, and Sue grabbed a sandwich in the coffee shop at the Millbury Arms. "Did you get a look at the committee when they went through the lobby? They know something."

The whole town seemed to know something. The hearing room was packed when they returned. Every-

143

one was there. Even . . . even Don's parents! He couldn't believe it. Nothing short of the end of the world would get his dad off that farm on a weekday! He caught their attention as he was hustled down the aisle by the incoming crush, but they were too far away to do anything but wave uncertainly.

Don had finally broken through to the front of the room and turned toward his seat. He swept a last look at the crowd. His eyes fell on an old man sitting ten rows back near the wall. That wild thatch of white hair . . . Al Hill! What was old Al Hill doing here? Al's eyes caught his, held them. The old highway designer nodded, just a tiny motion. Then he gave Don a tight little grin.

And suddenly Don knew who had been feeding information to Senator Sylvestro. They'd all thought the sour old man didn't give a damn about anyone but himself. Yet he'd risked his retirement to put Senator Sylvestro on the right track.

No doubt he'd gotten an agreement that he wouldn't be called to testify. Don't worry, Al, Don promised silently. Not even Hobie will hear about it. He met the old man's gaze for another instant, then smiled. Now Al knew that he knew, and that was enough. Don sat down.

Chief Stone was a worried man. He stumbled as he reached the witness table and dropped his cap as he caught himself.

Senator Alexander cleared his throat. "Chief, I have agreed to defer the questioning to Senator Sylvestro."

Stone's face turned to concrete.

Sylvestro's high-pitched voice was like a drill. "Chief Stone, you may be aware that an assistant of mine visited your department last week."

144

"I became aware of it after she left."

"Do you know what she was there for?"

"Not exactly."

Sylvestro held up a sheet of paper in one hand and Don's notebook in the other. "This is a list of incidents involving Donald Ellison during the past several weeks, and this is Ellison's notebook listing his claims of police harassment. They tally exactly."

Stone rubbed his chin. "I don't see how that proves anything."

"It proves that a long series of police incidents, which Ellison claims were harassment, did, in fact, occur exactly as he described them."

The chief was silent.

"Six of those incidents took place in a nine-day span, Chief. Not even John Dillinger was stopped that many times in so short a period."

Laughter swept the room.

"Let me ask you, Chief: Was this baiting of Ellison supposed to be some sort of warning?"

Stone seemed to crumple. "I'd rather not answer that without advice of counsel."

Alexander said, "The hearing can be adjourned while—"

"No, I'll withdraw the question. Anyway, as far as I'm concerned, he's already answered it."

"Objection!" Sid Harte burst out.

Alexander pointed the handle of the gavel at him. "Councilman, will you remember that you are a member of this committee, not a defense lawyer! Go on, Senator Sylvestro."

"Thank you, Mr. Chairman. Chief Stone, was it your idea to conduct this campaign of fear against young Ellison?"

"No!" Stone blurted out. Then he realized that that single word had given Sylvestro the opening he was looking for. The blood drained from the Chief's face.

"Then who made that request?"

The Chief twisted in the trap. As he spoke, his voice shook. "I've been a police officer for nearly twenty years, Senator. I've been a good one. The crime rate in this town has dropped, while it has gone up all over the state."

"Nobody denies that you have done a fine job for this city, Chief, but I must insist on an answer to my question."

The Chief's mouth went dry and he took a drink of water. Don could actually hear the glass rattle against his teeth.

"I can't answer you, Senator."

A gasp of surprise broke from the audience.

"Chief, I hope you realize that you are in serious trouble," Sylvestro pointed out. "I find Officer Mangrum's absence too much of a coincidence to swallow. We have pretty well substantiated Ellison's claim of police harassment. Now you are facing a charge of contempt of the State Senate by refusing to answer a question of this committee."

The chief gripped the edge of the table, his knuckles dead white. "Senator," he said, his voice quavering, "I must respectfully refuse to answer your question on the grounds that it may tend to incriminate me."

"You're taking the Fifth Amendment?" Sylvestro said as if he couldn't believe what he had just heard. "Do you realize you've just admitted there may have been criminal activity involved in what you've done?"

Chief Stone was silent, shaken; perhaps destroyed.

"Are you finished, Senator?" Alexander asked.

146

Sylvestro nodded. He didn't look like a man who had just proved his point. He looked ill.

Now came the moment the people in the hearing room had been waiting for, whether they admitted it or not.

"The Chair," said Senator Alexander, "calls Mr. Carleton J. Munroe."

Heads flew around and necks stretched. Then the shining bald dome of The Man Downstairs rose from a seat at the rear of the room. He edged out to the aisle and strode to the witness stand, looking neither right nor left. The long face wore an expression that could have been chiseled in rock. Not anger, not fear. Just determination. After everything that had been heard today, Don realized, The Man Downstairs still thought he was right.

The wide-shouldered figure in the tan suit raised his hand, muttered the swearing-in words, and sat down alone at the witness table.

"You are Carleton J. Munroe, Director of the Department of Streets?"

"I am."

"How long have you served the City of Millbury, Mr. Munroe?"

"Thirty-four years. First with the Department of Sanitation, then with the Water Department, then as head of the Department of Streets."

"Your record is well known, even at the state capital," Alexander said agreeably, "and if I may say so, it is an excellent one."

"Thank you, sir."

"I'd like to add to that," Sid Harte announced. "Carleton—Mr. Munroe—is one of the most effective administrators the city has."

147

"I'm sure we agree on that," Alexander answered with some annoyance, and with a hard look at Harte. "Now, Mr. Munroe, you are aware of why we are here, of course. Perhaps we can clear the air with a simple direct question. Is there now, or has there ever been, any macing in your department?"

"You mean since I've been there? I can't speak for my predecessors. And by macing, I assume you mean are employees threatened in some way."

"In any way."

"Threatened because they refuse to contribute to the party. Is that the question?"

Alexander looked baffled. "Yes."

"The answer is that there is no record whatsoever of anyone ever having been penalized because of noncontribution," Munroe said with satisfaction. He folded his arms across his chest, and the long chin jutted out.

"Oh, enough! Enough!" Senator Sylvestro's high voice burst out.

Alexander stared at him. "I beg your pardon?"

"Let me do the questioning, Jimmy. You're handling him like a Christmas-tree ornament."

Alexander's eyes blazed, but he said, "Very well. Proceed." He sat back, looking as though somebody had stolen his pet puppy.

Sylvestro, obviously tired of it all and probably already knowing the answers, pounced.

"Mr. Munroe, never mind what shows on your department records. Have you, in fact, laid off Donald Ellison?"

"No, he's on leave with pay."

"For how long?"

"No date has been set."

"Don't evade the question, Mr. Munroe. I saw the TV interviews Friday evening. I have talked with Mr. Pegler, your chief engineer, and with your personnel supervisor. Isn't it true that Ellison's pay stops when this hearing is over?"

"His leave stops then, yes."

"His pay, Mr. Munroe. His pay! When does it stop? Mr. Pegler had no trouble pinpointing the date. Why do you?"

Sylvestro's voice was a whiplash, reaching out, hitting hard. The hearing room buzzed, and Sue's fingers tightened on Don's arm. His throat was dry, and his heart thudded in his ears.

"Mr. Munroe, I asked you a question!"

Suddenly Munroe's neck flared red. He half stood and pointed a quivering finger at the sheaf of papers on the table at Sylvestro's elbow. "You have the answer there, along with all the other confidential information that my people have been feeding you! My *loyal* employees," he sneered. "I built that department into the city's best, you realize that? Now you can hardly wait to tear it down—you, Senator, and Crimm, Pegler, and Ellison, a naive kid who hardly knew what was going on." His words ran together as his voice rose.

The gavel banged. "Mr. Munroe, Mr. Munroe!" Alexander pleaded.

"And for what?" Munroe shouted, refusing to be silenced. "To be hauled up here and treated like a criminal!"

Alexander pounded, and the audience mutter grew into a roar. It drowned out Munroe's frantic shouting, drowned out even the sharp cracks of the gavel.

Then, like a wave breaking against rocks, the noise

receded. Munroe slumped in his chair, mopping his face with a bright-blue handkerchief. Even the Committee seemed drained.

Alexander brought his gavel down almost apologetically. "Gentlemen, need we take any more testimony?"

Sid Harte shook his head. Sylvestro said, "I think not."

"Then we are adjourned until four thirty this afternoon, when we will announce our findings." The committee members rose and left the room through a door near the head table. Munroe stood up slowly, glared at Don, then was swallowed up in the crowd.

"How about that?" Hobie said in Don's ear. "They're taking only an hour to deliberate."

"That means they've already made up their minds one way or the other," Don decided.

"Right, Sherlock. Any bets?"

Sue frowned. "You'd bet on a thing like this, Hobie?"

"When I think justice is about to be done."

"I think I'd better go say hello to my folks," Don said. "Sue, I know they'd like to see you, too."

The conversation with the elder Ellisons seemed to have barely begun when the gavel sounded. Don swung around. The committee was already seated. The room quieted so fast that it left everyone breathless.

"A formal written report will be submitted to the Governor's office for the record and to the Mayor's office for final action," Alexander announced. "This oral report is an informal summary of the committee's findings." He paused for a swallow of water.

"This has been a difficult situation for all of us, but we—Senator Sylvestro, Councilman Harte, and

150

myself—feel that its resolution is painfully obvious. There has indeed been political macing here, and there has also been purposeful police harassment. Therefore, we will recommend that Chief Glen Stone be brought up before the Board of Police Commissioners on a charge of misuse of police authority."

The room hummed.

"Further," Alexander said loudly to quiet the crowd, "we recommend that the Mayor relieve Carleton Munroe of his duties with the Department of Streets and that his successor be named within fifteen days."

The audience's mutter rose higher as The Man Downstairs abruptly stood and walked out. The gavel slammed.

"We have one final recommendation. Donald Ellison will be reinstated at the Department of Streets without prejudice of any kind appearing in his record. This hearing is now adjourned."

Reporters and photographers rushed up the aisle toward him, but Don ignored them as he reached for Sue and kissed her hard.

CHAPTER 19

By September, the Department of Streets had settled down. There had been changes, plenty of them. Billy Crimm was gone. Rumor had it that he'd gotten a job with some paper company over in East Millbury. Al Hill had been mysteriously granted his retirement benefits several months ahead of schedule, so he, too, had left.

Gil, Eddie Koslowski, and Kent Watters still worked at their old tables, but now Don was in the corner Al Hill had vacated. He had the prized "seat by the window, chair with a back on it." Newly promoted to chief engineer, Marty Corrigan lumbered from the glass office several times a week to give Don personal instructions in how to lay out roadway alignments. The work was fascinating.

Munroe, to everyone's surprise but Hobie's, had not made out badly. He was now director of the Millbury Planning Commission. "Would you believe it pays only five hundred bucks less per year than his job with the Department of Streets?" Hobie marveled.

And Chief Stone? He had been officially reprimanded by the Board of Police Commissioners, but he'd lost only a month's pay, not his job.

A bitter-sweet victory, Don decided. But life seemed to be like that. You never won everything. You had to make a few concessions.

On a quiet Thursday, Marty Corrigan leaned his bulk over Don's table. "The Man Downstairs wants to see you."

The Man Downstairs? He'd never thought of Munroe's replacement in that term. He laid down his pencil, walked down the wide steps, turned to follow the corridor to the rear of the building.

Munroe's hard-faced secretary had been replaced by a much softer blond girl. "Mr. Ellison? Go right in."

Charlie Pegler sat behind the big desk between the corner windows with his suit coat on and his World War II haircut neatly combed. "How do you like it, Don?" He grinned like a happy Airedale. "I had my own stuff put up just as soon as Munroe was out of here."

The displays of Munroe's mementos had been replaced by a scattering of framed photos of various Millbury scenes. "Those are all streets I helped design," Pegler said proudly. "Hey, sit down. I've got a couple of things to tell you."

Don took a chair near the desk. Pegler sat on a corner of the desk's polished surface.

"I owe you, Don," he said abruptly. "I'm not forgetting that."

"Owe me? You don't owe me a thing, Mr. Pegler."

"Charlie, Don. I'm Charlie to you from now on. Don't owe you! You're really something, Don. Don't you realize it was you who put me here? You got rid of Munroe!"

An odd feeling gripped Don. "I didn't go through all that to get rid of anybody, Mr.—"

"Charlie, Don. It's Charlie."

"I was trying to change a system I thought was unfair."

"Oh, I understand that. But nevertheless, he's gone, and I have the job. And it was you who made it happen. I don't forget my debts, Don. That's why I want you to be my personal assistant. There's a pay raise in it for you."

Taken totally by surprise, Don hesitated. "I'd planned to learn as much as I could upstairs—"

"Oh, you'd still be upstairs, Don. This would be an unannounced position."

"Unannounced?"

"Let's face it. I need a person up there I know I can trust."

Don stared, suspicion beginning to form. "Just what would the duties be?"

"Keep your eyes and ears open. Help out when the party needs support."

He couldn't believe what he was hearing. "You're asking me to be your Billy Crimm up there? And you want me to be your kickback collector?"

"No, no. It's going to be different from now on. No percentages of pay. Only a few banquet tickets now and then."

"Don't you see? That's the same thing. We'll have to buy tickets instead of kicking back part of our pay. What's the difference?"

Pegler attempted a smile. "You'll get to go to the banquets."

It was meant as a joke, but the time for joking had passed.

"Look, Don, I'm in the middle. The word has already come from you-know-where."

"The Mayor's office."

"I'd rather leave it fuzzy. The word is that the party needs support."

"The party will always need support."

Pegler held out his arms, palms up, in a hopeless gesture. "That's right. You just got the message. The people change, but the system goes on. But the trick is to learn to live with it the best way you can. I'm offering you a pretty darned good way."

The people change, but the system goes on. Pegler had stated the facts of Millbury life. There was only one way to handle this now.

Uneasy at Don's silence, Pegler prodded, "If you need a little time to wrestle with your conscience . . ."

"I don't need any time. I'm just wondering how to say it. I appreciate what you've done for me. And I guess you're offering me something you feel is a good break. But I can't accept it. In fact, I've just realized that I can't go on working here."

His voice was coming unglued, and he fought it. "This has to be my last day. I'll fill out an official resignation before noon, and I'll be out of here by closing time."

"Don—"

"I'm sorry, Mr. Pegler. That's the only way I can handle it."

He left Charlie Pegler, The Man Downstairs, standing in the middle of his new office, an odd expression breaking across his face. It began as surprise, but it slowly turned into something remarkably close to envy.

155

CHAPTER 20

"I ABSOLUTELY do not understand you!" Walter Wallace stormed. "First you turn the Department of Streets upside down. Then by some miracle you are snatched from the jaws of oblivion, offered a better position and an inside track. Now you've thrown the whole thing into the ashcan!"

He paced Don's living room, shaking his head. "Will somebody please tell me how you ever expect to survive in this world?"

"I guess you'll never see my side of it," Don said quietly, "and I can't explain it to you if you don't want to listen."

"I've listened."

"But you don't hear. Nobody hears. Not you." He turned to Elizabeth Wallace. "Not you." He looked at his wife sitting glumly beside her mother. "Sue?"

"I don't know what to think now. You don't have any job at all."

Useless. It was just useless to try to make these

people—anybody—understand why he had to do what he had done. From his first refusal to kick back part of his pay, he had known deep in his heart what would happen to him. He had known there was no other way. But it never seemed to end.

"Can't we all just—"

The door chime interrupted him. "Saved by the bell," he muttered without humor as he hurried into the entrance hall.

His father stood on the stoop in rumpled khaki trousers and a blue work shirt. Behind him in the parking lot Don spotted the old farm truck in which he himself had learned to drive.

Calvin held out a basket. "Tomatoes came in real good this year," he said clumsily. "I was bringing a load in to the wholesaler, and I thought you and Sue maybe could use some."

Don reached for the basket. "Sure, I guess we could." Strange, his father had never once visited him here before. "Want to come in?"

"Uh, no. I see you got company. Don't want to disturb you."

"It's only the Wallaces."

"No, I'll be getting along. Want to get downtown before dark."

He moved down the steps, then stopped. Don stood there awkwardly, the basket of tomatoes at his feet.

His father turned back, his face red. "Don't know how to say it, son. Words just won't come. I heard you quit."

"I couldn't stay there and see the same thing happen all over again. Maybe I was wrong, but I—"

His father rushed back up the steps and grabbed Don's hand in both of his. "No! No, you did right!

157

Remember I told you some sell out cheap, some sell out high. But you're one of them that don't sell out at all. By God, son, I'm proud of you!"

He swung around quickly, as if he didn't want Don to see his face. The gears screeched, and Don watched the old truck bounce out of the parking area.

He took a long breath of the early evening air. It smelled clean and fresh. He felt that way himself. He felt good. He didn't care what the Wallaces said to him now. Sue was the one he cared about, and he knew that before they moved out of Millbury, she would understand, too.